AS WORLDS DRIFTED

PARKER TIDEN

Cover by Mousam Banerjee instagram.com/illus_station

For A, A, and A

CONTENTS

PROLOGUE

If only that streak of light, the one burning across the sky, had been a falling star. I would have called it beautiful. But the fact that it was a rocket heading straight for me and my team, launched by some bastard intent on wiping us off the face of the planet, made me want to use a completely different adjective.

"We've got incoming!" Jarno yelled to my left as he scrambled for cover behind a tree—how quaint.

To my right, Girth and Nuffian sprinted towards some boulders. "Come on, Luna!" Girth shouted. "Get the hell down!"

I didn't move. I stood where I was, feet firmly planted in the dirt, fully exposed to what was coming at me. My trusted MP5 automatic was out of ammo, so I pulled the Magnum out of its holster and raised it in a two-handed stance. The short-barreled weapon's lack of accuracy was hardly ideal given the situation. I could only hope my skill would make up the difference.

"You're loco!" Nuffian shouted.

He was right. I was crazy. Not two months ago, I had been in a different world, in a different life. I hadn't known my team —Nuffian, Jarno, and Girth. I had never even touched a weapon. Then everything changed.

A familiar rage filled me as my jaw tightened in tandem with my grip on the Magnum. I took aim and held steady. Time slowed as the deadly projectile barreled towards us. I inhaled, held the air inside me, and pulled the trigger. There was a blast, and the heavens came raining down on us. Massive chunks of burning shrapnel pounded the earth and split the tree. One particularly irritating piece of shrapnel slammed into my shoulder, spun me around, and landed me face-down in the dirt. I slowly lifted my head and could see my three teammates as they came running towards me—they were alive. I rolled over onto my back and looked up at the evening sky. It was cobalt blue. The last time I had seen that blue, I was on the Pacific with my dad.

SNOW GLOBE

The only thing tethering us to earth was a sliver of carbon fiber. I was perpendicular to the water six feet below me as the wind flung us across the bay at over 25 miles per hour. I hung from the trapeze that connected my waist to the mast, with the tips of my sailing shoes the only part of me touching the hull. I gripped the rudder and felt the boat hum in frequency with the universe. My dad, in his yellow helmet, looked back at me with a wide grin on his face. I couldn't have known that this was the last time we would sail together.

We pulled up the Nacra 17 along the launch and parked the Olympic grade, hydrofoil, and twin trapeze-equipped, catamaran sailing boat in her spot alongside dozens of other sailing boats. I pulled off my helmet. Racing Nacras was no walk in the park. The speeds were so intense that any wipeout or collision could generate massive unpredictable forces. Helmets were mandatory under most racing conditions, as was carrying a knife, and body protection was recommended.

"Looking good out there, Lily," my sailing coach, Sylvester, greeted us outside the boathouse. "Your tacking was lightning fast."

"Thanks in large part to her crew," my dad laughed.

"The crew," I said, eyeing my dad up and down, "could stand to lose a few pounds."

Dad and I tried to get out on the water every Saturday morning. We'd missed the past few Saturdays because of his work, and now that I looked at him sitting behind the wheel as we drove home, he looked tired. I'd inherited his strong chin and straight nose, mine on and around which discreet freckles had begun to form after hundreds of days on the ocean. I had his chestnut hair—mine was longer, held up in a ponytail. His had started to salt and pepper on the sides like an earlier version of Clooney.

After we got back home, we were in the kitchen making sandwiches for lunch, and my dad had just told my mom that he needed to go to the office. Mom was, in some ways, a counterpoint to my dad's fundamental happiness and positivity. Her considerable beauty was increasingly confounded by bitterness. When she finally did smile, she smiled only with her mouth.

"What's going on?" my mom said as she grabbed the jar of mayo from my dad's hands. "What are you hiding?" she plunked the jar down on the marble countertop—I didn't know what would crack first, the jar or the countertop. "Are you having an affair?"

"You're kidding, right?" he said. "Honey, we've talked about this. I will tell you when I can. I promise," he moved in to hug her. "This is one of the last meetings. We're at a really sensitive juncture."

She nudged him off and turned away. As she stormed out of the kitchen, she mumbled, "Who the hell has meetings nowadays anyways? So pathetically archaic."

Dad looked deeply unhappy for a brief moment, before remembering that I was there. "Let's get those sandwiches made before we lose the mayo," he said.

Dad left for work a half-hour later, but before he left, he hugged me in the entryway. Not uncommon behavior for him, he spent hugs freely, but now he held on longer and squeezed tighter. When he let go, he took a box from the table and handed it to me. "Here, this is for you," he said. "I love you, my Luna." He called me Luna sometimes.

"I love you too, Dad," I said, looking for the tape seam on the box, "but you really don't need to be giving me presents."

"You can open it after I've left." He grabbed the car keys, "I'll be back later. Have fun tonight. I probably won't be home until you've left." He gave a small wave and a sorrow-tinged smile. Just before disappearing out the door, he stopped and turned back to me. "Luna, baby, don't be too hard on your mother. She's trying." He turned and was gone. I stood alone in the entryway, suddenly cold and small, while outside the summer air thickened.

Back in my bedroom, I shut the door behind me and sunk down onto my bed. The box lay heavy in my hands. I found the seam, sliced the tape with my thumbnail, and lifted the lid. I removed a protective foam and grabbed cold, smooth glass. I pulled the object out and the box fell away. In my hands was the most beautiful thing I'd ever seen. It was a large snow globe. Inside, rather than your typical snowman or dog playing in a winter landscape, was a moon. The moon, seemingly hovering alone in a liquid filled with swirling stars, was graceful in its own melancholy.

THE COVE

A little while later, I stood in front of the full-length mirror in my sports bra and body shorts. My days on the water had left their mark on my body. My legs and arms were a golden brown, while the rest of me was milk. The sailing, volleyball, and field hockey had defined my biceps, sculpted my shoulders, and toned my stomach. I looked like I could kick some serious ass.

On Monday, I would be walking up the steps of high school as a sophomore, but today, it was Saturday. Just as I pulled on some shorts, a tank-top, and my Asics, the doorbell rang. "I've got it!" I yelled as I bounced down the stairs and pulled open the front door.

"I'll just drop this here for later," Sarah said and threw a duffle bag into the entryway. She looked like she'd walked right off a Ralph Lauren shoot, with effortless beauty and grace. "Ready to burn?" she said.

We set off running side-by-side through the winding streets, lined with cypress and pine. As we got closer to the hills, the lots got bigger, as did the houses on them. We came to where the blacktop ended and the dust trails began.

"Fenton will be there tonight," Sarah said.

"Gee, thanks for that information," I put in an extra gear and pulled out in front of her as the trail narrowed, "not!"

Sarah was right on my heels, but I could hear on her breath that the afternoon heat was getting to her. "I'm just sayin'," she exhaled.

"You better not be trying to set me up with that doofus." The trail kept on getting steeper. My quads were on fire.

Suddenly, Sarah sprinted past me on my right. Like a mountain goat, she pushed off some rocks on the side of the trail and was in front of me. We were almost at the top; I could see the lookout bench in the clearing. I was eating her dust and it was pissing me the hell off. I dug deep, if Courtney Dauwalter can run 240 miles, I can run a measly five. The trail widened its last 200 feet as we sprinted out of the trees. My blood pounded through my temples as I glanced left. We were even with 50 feet to go. Sarah was pushing so hard, she looked like she was crying. Crying? Come on! Give me a break! I pushed ahead with 20 feet left. I wasn't gonna deviate from my mission to crush.

Then a memory came to me. Sarah waltzes up to me during morning recess, my first day in a new school, in a new town. In her wide-eyed blondness, with unfathomable confidence, she takes my eight-year-old hands in hers and declares that we were now friends forever. She saves me on what had started out as the worst day of my life and ended up being the best.

Sarah hit the bench. When she realized she was first, she forgot that she was supposed to be spitting blood. Instead, she broke out into an obnoxious dance. I was ready to keel over, trying to learn to breathe again with my hands on my knees.

Sarah stopped dancing. She stepped up on the bench and stretched out a hand to me. I joined her. We stood there, next to each other, in silence, our breathing still heavy but our minds light. In front of us stretched the bay, framed by the mountains and the city. The bay was glorious. I knew that she could also be treacherous, with her strong currents, unexpected winds, and unpredictable tourist boats.

Sarah turned to me and locked me in with her eyes, "If you ever let me win again on purpose, I'll kill you."

A couple of hours later, we were ready—in jeans shorts and tops. Halfway out the door, I shouted, "Mom! We're heading to the beach!"

"Phone!?" I heard from the upper reaches of the house.

"Duh, Mom!"

We pushed out into the warm evening, leaving the tension behind. Carl and his friend, Fenton, were leaning casually against Carl's battered car. "Ladies," Carl, in khaki shorts and a tight short-sleeved shirt with the top two buttons unbuttoned, held the shotgun door open for Sarah. Fenton, similarly but less successfully dressed, opened the backdoor for me. Ever since Sarah and Carl hooked up around Christmas, I'd been in a forced relationship of sorts with Fenton. He was mostly harmless.

Carl turned the key and the engine came to life, rumbling through my thighs. Fenton kept throwing glances my way. Sarah flipped down the makeup mirror. "You better keep your grubby hands off her, you hear me? I'll be watchin' you," she said. Carl turned up the stereo and the summer beats took us all the way to the beach.

The fire sprung to life as someone flicked a match into the pile of twigs and driftwood. The orange sun hung on the horizon as if suspended in disbelief at its own beauty, ready to tuck in for the night and make way for the moon. They were all there, Sarah, Carl, Fenton, and a dozen or so more of the gang. We were far out on a lip of land stretching out into the Pacific, barefoot in still-warm sand.

Music, competing with the waves, pumped out of a Bluetooth speaker stuck in the sand. We danced and laughed, partying like we could make summer last forever if we just wanted it desperately enough. Sarah and Carl were intertwined, and Fenton was still right beside me, where he had been all night. He wasn't all that bad despite his horrendous white man boogie moves. The fact that he didn't care what others thought of him was cute—maybe even a smidgeon attractive.

It was dark now, except for the moon and the last of the embers from the campfire, around which we had settled. I looked over at Sarah, sitting on the other side of the fire with her head on Carl's shoulder. She grinned and gave me a knowing nod. We both got up. "We'll be back," she said as we walked away from the fire together. We walked in silence towards some house-sized rocks at the far end of the beach. It couldn't have been more than a few hundred feet from the fire. As we reached the rocks, a gap revealed itself. "No second thoughts?" Sarah asked.

"Are you kidding!" I said. Sounding more confident than I was, I pushed through the gap first, leaving the beach and our friends behind. On the other side, calm enveloped us. We'd been here before, but never at night. The cove was surrounded by rocks with an opening at the bottom connecting it to the ocean, and one upwards, letting the light from the gibbous moon pass through and bounce off the silky black water. The water was heaving with the ocean swell, like the slow breathing of some prehistoric creature.

Without saying another word, we took off our sweaters and tops, then pulled off our shorts. We were standing together in our underwear at the water's edge. We held hands, and together, we counted, "Three! Two! One!" and jumped. The Pacific in this part of the world is cold, water barreling down from the Arctic with the California current. I knew this, and still, as I broke the surface and plunged into the water, my lungs shrink-wrapped and my brain froze as my heart stopped and I sank into darkness. As the ocean tugged at me like a magnet, I opened my eyes, salt met salt, and I saw the moon above me recede —a blurry pale dot. My hand held nothing… Sarah was gone. I kicked upwards towards the surface and got nowhere.

I'm only 12 on the day I almost die. I've just gradu-ated from dinghies to catamarans. It's late October, whitecaps stretch across the bay. I have a wetsuit on under my sailing gear against the cold, my fingers are stiff under my gloves. A second of inattention, a failure to release the boom at the right mo-ment, and I flip. The catamaran's mast slams into the water and I catapult off. I hit the water and go under. For a second, I don't know where I am, then I see the light of day above me and swim towards it. I'm almost at the surface, ready to fill my lungs with air, when I'm yanked back. I try again but get yanked back even harder. I look down, a rope from the mast, which is pointing straight down into the depths, is wrapped around my ankle. The harder I tug, the more the rope tightens around me. I start to panic, my lungs about to explode, the surface just out of reach. I can't think straight. I'm all instincts, and they're just making things worse. My field of vision narrows, my world going dark. Then I see from above, something red breaks the surface and I feel someone grab me under my arms and pull me. Finally, I break the surface and gasp. Cold air and life rush into me. I'm pulled up out of the water into a boat and I lie on the deck on my side and cough up half the Pacific.

Sylvester saved my life that day. He'd been on the water in the chase boat, and he dived right in when he saw me go under. He cut the rope with a knife. After the incident, the school upped its act and contracted with a former navy diver to teach us to hold our breaths for more than four minutes and to use a knife underwater. Of course, Sarah had none of that training.

I broke the surface and air rushed into my lungs. I was alone. I looked down into the dark water, and just below me, so close I could almost touch her with my feet, was Sarah. Her blond hair fanned out in the water like the always beautiful, young, female murder victims on crime shows. I dove down. When I got to her, I could see only the white of her eyes, wide with fear. I gave her a thumbs-up, a vain attempt to calm her, circled back around, and wrapped an arm around her from behind.

Seconds later, we lay next to each other on the smooth wet rock in the dark, shivering, desperately filling our lungs. For a second, I thought Sarah was crying, but then I heard it for what it was—laughter. I couldn't resist her, and we lay there for way too long in hysterical laughter at the joy of being alive, at the triumph of sticking it to the man of all men—death. My body sang, like a pitchfork in tune with what all that there is, and ever will be. It could never get any better than this.

A figure came running towards us on the beach as Sarah and I, huddled together for warmth, emerged from the gap. It was too dark to see who it was. The figure stopped, turned back towards the campfire, and shouted, "They're here! I've found them!" I recognized the voice, it was Fenton. "Where were you guys?"

"Oh, we just went for a little swim," Sarah said, trying for nonchalance but not really nailing it. I giggled, still giddy.

"What did you two smoke?" Fenton asked, "Magic sea-weed?"

At the campfire, I went for my bag to find some jeans, I was still shaking cold. As I pulled it open, I saw light inside. It was my phone. I pulled it out, and for the first time in hours, I checked it. I had missed five calls and six messages, all of them from my mom. The last message read "CALL PLEASE!!!" I checked the time, which was now slightly past 1 am. It had been sent an hour ago. Mom wasn't a worrier by nature, she was rarely on my case when it came to my extra-curricular activities—I had never given her cause. I kept my grades well up, was a pretty good athlete, and my friends were polite (at strategic moments at least). Besides, it wasn't really that late considering that this was the last party before school starts. I called her back but it went straight to voicemail. I dialed my dad, which also went unanswered.

I grabbed my bag and stepped away from the fire for a second and took in one deep breath, studied the scene and the joy on my friends' faces as if I wanted it to be etched into my brain, and turned around.

My heart pounded as I hurried through the bushes, guided by the moonlight, to the main road. I ordered an Uber on the fly, it would be five long minutes according to the app. I sent off a quick message to Sarah—no time for goodbyes. As I reached the main road, I spotted lights streaking low across the sky from behind a hill. I prayed that it was the Uber I had ordered.

The Tesla stopped when it saw me, I jumped in and nodded to the driver. He didn't say a word, thank God. In silence, we drove through the hills. After what felt like forever, but probably wasn't more than 15 real minutes, the Uber rounded the corner to our street. The houses were dark, the neighbors asleep in their upper-middle-class cocoons. I could see lights up ahead, strobing lights, blue and red, lighting up my house. My phone buzzed, it was a text from Sarah, what's wrong!!

Yellow tape stretched across the street between two cypress trees stopped us. A cop with a big black gun strapped across his chest signaled the Uber to turn around. I told the driver to stop, and I stepped out of the car. The streetlight lit the cop from above, casting his eyes in shadow.

"Step back, nothing to see here," he said, gripping his gun.

"That's my house," I said anxiously, pointing to the house with all the lights on inside, and cops walking in and out, milling around outside.

"ID," he requested, putting his gloved palm forward and motioning with his fingers.

"I don't have ID, and I don't need one to get to my own house!"

He pointed a flashlight in my face. "What's your name?"

"Lily," I said, squinting. "Lily Anderson."

"Wait here," he said and turned sideways as he spoke into the radio on his chest. "We've got the daughter here."

"I need to get to my house," I cried, my throat tightening. "Where's my mom and dad?!" I went for the tape.

He blocked me and grabbed me by the shoulder. "Stand back!"

My jaw tightened and fist clenched. I yelled, "What are you gonna do? Shoot me?!" I started for the tape again, the cop looked like he was about to body slam me.

"Let her through," a voice came from behind the wall of a cop. "It's her house after all." I rounded the cop and lifted the tape. "Hi, Lily," a man in a suit, the source of the voice, came towards me. "I'm agent Maxwell, FBI."

"Where are they?"

Gum churned in his mouth, "I'm afraid we've got a bit of a

situation."

THE RUMBLING OF
JET ENGINES

I 'd never been afraid of flying. The rumbling of jet engines, the roar of the air being pushed out of the way at 800 miles an hour, all filtered through the plastic and aluminum (or titanium or whatever planes are made of) of an airliner's body, was comforting. To sit on the cusp of the atmosphere with the promise of transformation. That rumbling, that roar, I felt it now again. Only, this time, I was on the ground, nowhere near an airliner. The sound was inside me. My blood was roaring through my brain, my soul imploding into my stomach.

What was agent Maxwell saying? I couldn't grasp. No more than twelve hours earlier, I had stood in this entryway in my father's embrace before he turned and stepped out.

My mom was at the kitchen table when I walked in. Her face was blank, her stare empty. It wasn't until a few days later that the picture of what happened that night became clear to me. It went something like this. At approximately 10 pm, there's a loud knock on our front door. I'm at the party on the beach. Mom, alone at home, opens the door. A dozen FBI agents stand on the doorstep with a federal search warrant. Mom is powerless to stop them, so they proceed to forcefully, and recklessly, search the entire house. Mom frantically calls and texts my dad, whom she thinks is at work, but the calls go to voicemail and the texts are unanswered.

At around 11 pm, word comes through cop radio that a

car has been found idling outside the offices of Westcap Envir-oTech. An unidentified male is in the driver's seat, seemingly asleep or unconscious. The car doors are locked. When the cops smash the window, they discover that the male is, in fact, pulse-less—dead. At 12.30 am, the body is conditionally identified as a 43-year-old male by the name of Sam Anderson, beloved husband, and devoted father of one. The cops don't take any chances and immediately deem our house a secondary crime scene, even before they know the cause of death. The last of the cops don't leave the house until 7 am.

When they finally left, my mom was still at the kitchen table, walled off by grief or anger, or a mixture of both. The house looked like it had been bombed. I was in a daze. I couldn't stay in the kitchen with a mom incapable of providing or re-ceiving comfort, so I ventured out into the house and ended up in my dad's study.

Dad's computer, fixed-line phone, and all his papers were gone. Books and other debris lay strewn across the floor. I bent down and picked up a framed picture of an eight-year-old me and dad smiling, holding up my third-place medal from my first club sailing competition. The frame's glass was shattered, as was my dad's favorite tea mug—a monstrosity I'd made in sec-ond grade. My room was barely in better shape.

Those first few weeks after his death were hued in darkness, and revealed themselves, afterwards, only in a few blurred vi-gnettes. People had come to the house, but I didn't come down to see them. My cell rang and beeped and alerted. I threw it against the wall and it exploded into pieces.

The darkness was compounded by the developing inves-tigation. The FBI agent, Maxwell, the same agent that had first met me outside the house, came over at least half a dozen times over the next few weeks. I had to sit down for an interrogation. Maxwell churned his gum and asked about my dad.

It became clear pretty fast that the feds weren't inter-ested in how he died. For them, it was an open and shut case of suicide. What they wanted to know was what he had done before he died.

Had I noticed anything unusual in the months, weeks, days, or hours before his death? No.

Had he been acting differently lately? No.

Had he met people outside his usual orbit? Not that I know of.

Had he given anything to me recently? No, I lied reflexively.

The investigation and the delayed death certificate meant that the funeral didn't take place until several weeks after he died. My mom kept the funeral to close family only. At the funeral, I couldn't cry.

Someone in the FBI was leaking like a White House staffer. The local newspapers and TV stations framed my dad as an embezzler, a white-collar criminal, who when the law was closing in on him, took the easy way out. The final police report didn't, in the end, deviate much from the media report. The official version went something like this:

Mr. Anderson gets word of the ongoing raid on his house.

Mr. Anderson fires off an email to his wife, with a simple message—*I'm sorry.*

Mr. Anderson leaves the office and heads for the parking lot.

Mr. Anderson gets in his car and locks the doors.

Mr. Anderson downs a handful of assorted pills with a bottle of Macallan whisky.

Mr. Anderson passes out.

Mr. Anderson dies.

All this might be plausible to someone who didn't know Mr. Anderson. I knew Mr. Anderson. Mr. Anderson was my dad.

"Let me see here," the lady on the other end of the line said. "Says here that the report is sealed."

"What do you mean, sealed?"

"You're right, Miss Anderson. Ordinarily, next-of-kin can

access the autopsy report. But this particular report has been sealed by order of the federal district judge. There isn't much I can do for you at this juncture. May I suggest you contact your lawyer."

Why all the secrecy? It was just all too convenient. Why would you want to hide the autopsy report of someone who has killed themselves?

This was the latest in a long string of setbacks. What enraged me more than anything was that my mom was buying the whole thing, the official version, hook, line, and sinker. I said we needed to hire a private investigator to help us, but she said we didn't have the money. I said, "Well, sell the house." She said no.

One of the sucky things about dying while under federal investigation is that you never get your day in court—not a court in this dimension anyway. The cloud of suspicion around you lingers on into eternity. I knew that what they were accusing him of was ridiculously wrong. With no outlet, my hate festered.

Speaking of hate, agent Maxwell had insinuated himself into our lives. Those first few weeks, he kept on showing up at the house with care packages, or pizzas, telling us that he was on our side, trying to dig up any information, any piece of the puzzle that could help us get to the truth. He had roped in my mom, exploiting her inherent vulnerability to peddle his lies.

One afternoon, the last time he visited the house, as the investigation was wrapping up, I came down from my room to find him sitting with my mother at the kitchen island. It looked so horrifyingly mundane. I tried to turn back to my room, but I'd been spotted.

"Hey, kiddo, how you holding up?" Maxwell said, still chewing that gum of his.

I walked over to the kitchen counter without offering an answer. I turned my back to them as I filled the electric kettle.

"Lily, we've got some tea already made over here," my mom said.

I pulled out my favorite mug from the cupboard. I wasn't a

fan of teabags, they were for amateurs, but they could be useful when you're in a hurry.

They realized pretty quickly that they weren't going to get a word from me, so they continued as if I weren't there. "We've established that he stole the money," he paused as he sipped from his tea. "But we can't find it, and as long as the money is missing, the judge won't let up." He sighed as though he really cared, "They will take everything you own." If I turned around and saw his hand touching my mom's, I would jam the meat cleaver between his eyes. The cleaver stood in its stand, mere inches away from me.

"We have nothing," my mom pleaded. "There is no money."

"Oh, I believe you, but it's the federal judge you need to convince."

"Is there anything you can do?"

I poured boiling water into the mug and grabbed milk from the fridge. I still had my back turned to them, but I was pretty sure that he was shaking his head in false pity just about now. I poured the milk into the tea, before it had finished infusing, and was out of there. That would turn out to be the last time I saw Maxwell, for a while.

First day of sophomore year came and went. First week of sophomore year came and went. I hardly left my bedroom, going days without talking to anyone. For now, the system was leaving me alone, any school district representative or truancy officer knocking on my bedroom door were probably weeks away. Considering all the commotion the case had created, the school must have been relieved that I stayed away.

My mom had her own issues, dealing with feelings of loss and betrayal, or whatever she was dealing with. If my mom was on psychotropic drugs before this all went down, she must have doubled or tripled her dose. If she had been a distant mother before, she was in her own orbit now—an orbit around another star, in another corner of the Milky Way.

A few weeks after his death, I opened the fridge and thought I saw something move. It became increasingly clear that my mom's hands-off approach to homemaking and child-rearing wasn't really working out, and that I would have to pick up the slack at home. The feds had frozen my dad's assets, but by some miracle, someone over there wasn't doing their job because the credit card on FreshDirect was still alive and ticking. I could go online and order whatever we needed, which wasn't much, with the added bonus of not having to step outside the house.

Electricity and water were still on, but I could see the pile of bills on the hall table growing day by day. I knew the days in this house, our house, were numbered.

One night, I sat in front of the mirror in my room. In my face I saw him, his eyes in mine. My foundations, lipsticks, eyeliners, cotton swabs, eyeshadows, rouges, perfumes, tweezers, hairbrushes, and myriads of creams, all lay spread out as I had left them on the night of the last party, the night he died. I grabbed the wastebasket off the floor with one hand, and with the other, I wiped the table clean of it all, the flotsam of my life as it had been.

I stared at myself again, my chestnut hair hung limp and greasy from days of neglect. The hair too, once a source of pride and self-definition, now seemed unnecessary and stupid. I rescued a pair of scissors out of the wastebasket and let them wander across my scalp, felling tuft after tuft until there were no more tufts to fell. The darkness under my eyes was now my most striking feature.

NICK

The first three weeks of my sophomore year at high school had come and gone without me setting my foot there. I didn't want to deal with the false pity in people's eyes. My mom told me that Sarah, Carl, and Fenton, and others, including teachers, dropped by the house. I refused to see them. In a moment of weakness, I opened up Snapchat on my Mac; messages and missed calls flooded the screen—most of them from Sarah. Most of them were from the first two weeks, and then they dropped off to a trickle.

You could say that I was feeling sorry for myself, maybe, but I just didn't see the point of it all. I spent most of my time staring at the ceiling of my bedroom, haunted by his death and by a feeling I couldn't shake... a feeling that something was seriously not kosher.

I knew that Nick Stranton lived in the house next to ours and had done so for years. Nick was my neighbor, but our circles had never really intersected. I saw his room from my window, through the tree, a California buckeye that separated our houses. There probably wasn't more than 20 feet between us, in this what used to be a working-class neighborhood.

In those still muggy September nights, when sleep no longer came, I would often see the blue light of a screen flicker in his room through my open window. One night, as I sat on my window ledge breathing in the still air, trying to catch a glimpse of the crescent moon, Nick's silhouette appeared suddenly in his window. I threw myself down on the floor of my room, not wanting him to think that I was spying, and, more to the point, not wanting him to strike up a conversation or something. I valued my isolation. Then I heard him say, "We should celebrate," through the tree.

I stayed down, hoping he hadn't seen me and that he was talking to someone else.

"Hey, Lily, want to celebrate?"

God, why can't he stop? I lifted my head slowly and, still on my knees, peered out into the night, and to my dismay, saw that he was staring right at me. I stood up and attempted casual, "Damn, can't find my contact... what were you saying?"

"I just got in my ten thousandth headshot, thought it might be worth celebrating."

I wasn't following his geek-speak. "You did what?"

"I play a lot of computer games, you know, and it's fun when you notice that you're getting better."

"I'm sorry, Nick, but really, I don't know what the hell you're talking about."

Nick hesitated for a second, "I know these weeks have been tough... I can't imagine..."

"No, you can't," I said as I started to slide my window shut.

"You're missed at school, you know. People are even asking me about you as if I know you. Nice haircut, by the way." Nick was backlit and several feet away, but from what I could remember, he looked like boys do nowadays. Through the foliage, I could glimpse carelessly tussled brownish hair, not dissimilar to mine in color, or at least what mine had been before I lopped it all off. It was hard to get a grasp of his face. His voice was kind, though.

"It's late. You too need to catch some sleep," I shut the window and drew the curtains.

The next night, I let the window stay shut with the curtain drawn, even though I hated not getting the air and a chance to see the moon, but I didn't want to risk having another conversation with another human being, let alone Nick. A while later, as I lay wallowing in my bed, staring at the proverbial ceiling, I heard a tap on my window. I sat up, then another tap, then a few seconds later, a third. Jesus, what the hell does that guy want now? I got up, pulled the curtain, and slid open the window, ready to rip into him.

"Listen Ni—" Something hit me square between the eyes.

"Oops"

I looked up and saw Nick standing in his window holding what could only be a nerf gun. In a split-second act of self-preservation, I picked up whatever happened to be closest to me and whipped it out the window and through the tree branches.

Nick yelled, "Whaaa! Are you nuts? Your countermeasure is hardly proportionate." He ducked down and re-emerged with an object in his right hand. At first, I couldn't make out what it was, but then I saw it. It was my snow globe—the snow globe with a moon in it that my dad had given me the day he died. I could lie for hours staring into the globe as the moon appeared to float in the glass with the stars whirling around it like the mother of all star-falls.

"Sorry, I acted instinctively, blame my genetic coding," I apologized. "Would you mind just tossing that thing back to me?"

"I think I'll keep it."

Cheeky bastard! Who does this nerd think he is? "Listen, Nick, just toss it over. I'm not in the mood."

"Tell you what. Why don't you drop by my house tomorrow afternoon and pick it up? Wouldn't want to risk breaking it, would we."

Before I could answer, or throw anything even more lethal at him, he closed his window and pulled the blind.

I had to wait the whole day for Nick to get back from school. It was excruciating. I was basically wearing the same thing I had been wearing since my dad died—a ratty pair of jeans and one of his college sweatshirts. I smelled of him. I hadn't even bothered to put on a pair of shoes as I ran across the lawn towards Nick's house. This, paired with my buzz cut, must have been a real shocker.

Nick opened his front door with a smile rather than a smirk, "Come on in, my parents are still at work." He seemed totally unfazed by the way I looked. I should have knocked him out cold then and there, but I wanted to get my snow globe first. Besides, that smile went well with his face. His eyes were blue.

"That won't be necessary, just hand over what's mine."

"Possession is nine-tenths of the law."

"Just hand it over."

"First, come in and check out my setup."

"What the fu—"

"My *computer* setup," he sighed.

Whatever I need to do to get back what is mine. I reluctantly followed him up the stairs. Why does he think I would give a crap about his computer setup? On his desk, he had a total of three monitors. What a mega nerd. It was surprisingly clean for a gamer's room, not that I'd ever been in one. No lingerie models on the walls, no empty pizza boxes scattered across the floor, and the air was more or less breathable.

He pointed to the wall opposite the window, there was a large dent where the drywall had caved in.

"No way," I said, cheeks burning.

"Yes way. You're loco, lady. Speaking of loco, I've got just the fix for you, sort of like anger management class," he said, motioning to the desk chair. "It's called Alphacore."

"I don't have time, Nick, just give me the globe," besides, that chair was probably in violation of scores of health codes anyhow.

"From what I can tell, you have nothing but time, Lily, and it's slowly killing you."

"Whatever, Dr. Jung."

"Just sit."

"Please, Nick, just hand me the globe. Don't try to socialize me, let me crawl back under that rock where I came from. I like it under that rock."

"Fine, here," Nick tossed the globe and pointed towards the door. "You don't know what you're missing." He actually looked disappointed for real.

Whatever, it won't kill me, I don't think. "Ten minutes, that's all I got," I sighed and plunked down in front of his screens. "There seems to be something wrong with your screen here. Did it like melt in the sun or something?"

"Funny... it's curved. Improves immersion—at least for first and third-person shooters. It's the latest Samsung, refresh rate of 240. Set me back more than 500." Seeing my eyes glaze over, he stopped talking and put a set of over-ear headphones on me and slid a transparent visor down over my eyes. The screen came to life as the pixels crackled in tandem with my synapses. "The visor has two functions," Nick continued in his irritating geek-speak. "It further enhances immersion by creating an illusion of presence, and it picks up your facial expressions, which allows realistic interaction with other players."

"You sound like a used car salesman."

"Enough theory, time for practical application. We're gonna take it slow. First, you'll just learn to move around in the world." He leaned forward from behind me and took my right hand, blood rushed to my head as my spine tingled. "You hold the mouse with this one." He seemed unaware of the intimacy of his gestures, and that I'd basically touched no one for weeks. "Left hand on the WASD keys here on the keyboard."

"The what keys?"

"W-A-S-D keys. You use them to move around. This keyboard cost more than two Benjamins."

"Oh, I'm sure it did, look, it has all these extra buttons and pretty colors."

Nick continued to ignore my jabs, "The left mouse button you use to fire your weapon, right mouse button to turn. Spacebar to jump. Control to duck. You'll be playing one of my alt characters, wouldn't want anything to happen to Nuffian."

"Nuffian?"

"He's the character I play with... my avatar."

"Couldn't find a better name? You know, like Lancelot or Maximus Prime, or Legolas?"

Nick took over the mouse again and rapidly scrolled through various menus. "Here, take SoomoBrother. He's really good with a hunting knife, and pretty dependable with a standard rifle. He won't let you down."

What must have been SoomoBrother appeared on the screen. He looked a bit like a hunter with elven ears. "Sure, sounds fine." God, what a nerd. Speaking of his character as though he were real. "But whether he is dependable or not must depend on how I play him, right?"

Nick pressed a button on the keyboard and, suddenly, in front of me was a landscape of detailed beauty, with tall grass swaying in waves of wind on rolling hills. SoomoBrother had his back turned to me and was taking in the same landscape as I was. Trees dotted the prairie giving some perspective towards the towering snowcapped mountains in the distance and the clouds that swirled among the peaks. I felt Nick place his right hand over mine and push down my ring finger with his, and as he moved the mouse slightly to the left, the prairie turned with it as SoomoBrother turned. I was suddenly facing the other direction with the mountains to my back and a gurgling stream with an accompanying stone bridge in front of me.

"Press and hold W," Nick said from behind me. I did as he said, and SoomoBrother started to walk towards the stream.

"What happens if I go in? Does SoomoBrother drown?" I didn't wait for an answer. The water swirled around his legs as he struggled through the swift water before he emerged on the other side. He didn't fall, or drown.

I looked up at the sky. There was a moon. Wait, there were two... three... four moons. One looked to be five times the size of our moon. Our moon? Somehow, I managed to hit the shift button and I started to run. I tried the rest of the WASD keys, moving left, right, and backwards. At first, my left-hand/right-hand coordination was seriously flawed. More often than not, I

23

wasn't facing the way I was moving, causing me to hit objects such as trees and boulders. Eventually, I got the hang of it and could use the mouse to turn my head in the same direction I was moving—what a relief.

I had left the stream and prairie behind. A forest of white and gray birch trees enveloped me; the odd birdsong punctuated the comforting silence. A rustle in the undergrowth and out into a clearing, not 20 feet from me, stepped a fawn—or this world's approximation of one. It scraped a hoof along the ground and bent down to nibble on whatever root it had exposed, oblivious to my existence.

I left the fawn behind and found a path that led to a dirt road, which led to what looked like a village. The village was abandoned, most of the windows were broken, and doors swung eerily on their hinges. A godforsaken church rose in the middle of the village. I navigated the scattered tombstones, and against my basic survival instincts, proceeded to pull open the church doors. I stepped through the foyer, where dusty prayer books with red covers lay in piles on the stone floor, and entered the sanctuary. The sun slanted through what was left of the tall windows, highlighting dozens of pews strewn about as though God had decided to play Mikado. Suddenly, behind me, I heard footsteps and the door pushed open.

"Lily? Hey, Lily..." I felt something touch my shoulder. I whipped around, the hunting knife in my right hand, ready to kill, but saw nothing. I felt a touch on my shoulder again, so I whipped around the other way, crouching, ready to pounce.

"Hey, Lil..." I shot out of the chair, ripping the headphones off my head. In front of me stood Nick. "I'm glad you like it and all, but it's ten. I actually have a meet-up in Alphacore to get to."

"What?!" Did he leave at some point and eat dinner and come back without telling me? Whatever happened, I'd just wasted five hours of my life, and it was time to go.

"I gotta run," I said, already halfway out the door.

"You forgot something!"

Shit! I spun around, swooped up the snow globe, and hurried home.

TRISTAN CASCO

"Here you are, hun," the waitress smiled as she slid a plate in front of him with one hand, and poured coffee with the other. "Your eggs will be out in a minute."

"Thanks, Maggy." Tristan Casco always found comfort in diners—an oasis of simplicity in a world that felt increasingly alien. Tristan sighed as he poured milk powder into his coffee.

A little while later, Tristan over-tipped and stood up, trying not to wince as pain shot through his right leg. He threw on his suit jacket and headed out the door just as the first faint rays of day hit this rundown part of town, where auto repair shops and tattoo parlors had yet to make way for bearded vegans and their microbreweries. A block or two down the street, Tristan swiped his card and glanced up into the camera that was carefully concealed in the wall above him. The nondescript half-rusted door in front of him slid open, and he stepped in as it hissed shut behind him. He grabbed the rail as the floor dropped, and he was whisked to the floors below. He stepped out onto the landing and took in the scene that never failed to contribute to his alienation.

Below him stretched a large bustling room with high ceilings and rows of computer workstations. With massive screens on the walls, the room looked a lot like mission control at Cape Canaveral. Tristan walked on down to his workstation, doing his best not to limp. Maria Castillo was already at her station to his right, as was Frank Weber to his left.

"What've we got?" Tristan asked as he sank into his chair in front of his six monitors, two rows of three.

"You know, your usual money laundering, embezzlement, human trafficking, and a smattering of terrorist chatter," Maria answered without looking up.

Tristan put on his headset and flipped down the visor. He typed some commands into the keyboard, which incidentally wasn't the typical gamer keyboard, it had at least twice the number of keys and a couple of built-in mini-LCDs.

He glanced out across the room at the dozens of people playing computer games. The average age of these nerds couldn't be more than 22. Tristan was by far the oldest tool in the joint, with the possible exception of the janitor. Towards the front of the room was the Moba cluster—the agents surveilling the multiplayer online battle arena games such as League of Legends, Heroes of the Storm, Smite, and Dota 2. In the middle were the ultra-nerds who followed card games like Hearthstone and Magic: The Gathering. At the back, where his team was seated, were the first and third-person shooters like Overwatch, Counter-Strike, Team Fortress, Fortnite, PlayerUnknown, and, of course, Alphacore Legacy.

This was the FBI Cyber Gaming Unit HQ, in the heart of Silicon Valley. Together, Maria, Frank, and Tristan made up the Alphacore Legacy Task Team. As more and more human communication took place through these online gaming platforms, the federal government had seen a need to bolster its own presence in these communities. So, this had become Tristan's fate, to sit on his ass all day with a bunch of kids and pretend to enforce the nation's laws while playing computer games.

It wasn't his choice. He'd never been a gamer as a kid. He'd been the sports kid. But once his leg was shattered on a mission a few years back, he'd been placed in this hell hole. His lack of computing experience had proven to be downright embarrassing when he had first started at the CGU. They had to send him for three weeks of nerd boot camp.

Despite his lack of gaming experience, he started out as

team leader. Maria and Frank had taken the whole thing well enough. Tristan liked to believe that he contributed to creating a cohesive and balanced team, and for the past half a year, their Alphacore team had been among the top performers in the unit.

Tristan had taken the skills he had learned on the street and brought them online. He had pioneered the use of paid informants. Even the young nerds at the CGU were required to go through the basic FBI training at the academy in Quantico, though it was tailored to their specific needs. The agents at the CGU did pack heat, but they rarely got to unpack said heat. Tristan felt it was his duty to make sure that his team was up to par, so he would take them to the shooting range to top up their firearm skills and organize supplementary hand to hand combat training. He even took them on a weekend of advanced interrogation techniques. All the things you can do in your free time when you don't have kids—of course, Tristan did have a kid, he just wasn't allowed to see much of her nowadays.

Bots were anathema to any gaming community. Fairness principles were central, and any suspicion that the game was rigged somehow could be a serious threat to any game company. The gaming industry had spent millions on Capitol Hill to block federal law enforcement's push to get federally controlled bots into the online games. They had failed. So, a good part of intelligence gathering, and even interaction with the community, took place through bots. These were carefully designed bots stuffed with the latest artificial intelligence, which allowed them to convincingly (most of the time) mimic human social interaction. But, sometimes, you just needed to get your hands dirty.

DREAMS OF DAD

Sleep was a mess. My synapses were still firing on over-drive. It was as if I had finally been awoken from my grief-induced cerebral slumber with a Pulp Fiction syringe of pixelated adrenaline right to the brain. In the weeks since my dad's death, my sleeping life had been working in tandem with my waking life to create a pitch-black nothingness. Every night when I fell asleep, I was sucked into a dreamless void. I guess I should have been thankful not to be wracked by nightmares.

But that night, after having tried Nick's game, I revisited Alphacore in my sleep. I revisited the prairie, the stream, the mountains, and the forest. Then, suddenly, before me, I saw him. In the distance, on the top of a hill, sitting under a great tree was my dad. He looked out over the fields before him, like I had seen him do hundreds of times before on the sea, the wind through his chestnut hair. I shouted, I waved, I cried, I tried to run to him, but got no closer. He began to fade, to pixelate, and then he was gone.

My first time in Alphacore, and my strong reaction to it, scared the hell out of me. I had lost control, and I hated losing control. So, when I saw the flickering blue light in Nick's window that next night, I made sure to close the curtains and make myself scarce. Nick seemed to have gotten the message, or maybe I had freaked him out too, and he made himself just as scarce over the next few days. There was one major problem with this avoid-ance strategy. After that first night, I stopped dreaming again. I missed the dreams. I needed to see my dad again.

Two more dreamless nights, and I couldn't take it anymore. I sat in my window and waited for Nick to get home from school. As soon as I saw movement in his window, I threw some beads at it.

"Well, well, what do you know," Nick said with an irritating grin as he pulled open his window. "I was just wondering when you'd come back for more."

This was not a little embarrassing... groveling did not come naturally. "Yeah, well, I uhh..."

"Come on over. I was just about to boot up."

A few minutes later I was in Nick's gaming chair again. The Alphacore logo rotated enticingly on his curved monitor.

"What you experienced the other day was just the beginning, believe me," Nick said as he leaned over me to type in a few commands. "Today, we're gonna take it to a whole other level. Today, we're gonna teach you how to kill."

"Oooh, this should be really neat," I said, feigning indifference. But the fact was, I couldn't wait. I put on the headphones, flipped down the visor, and found myself in SoomoBrother again. I moved the mouse and took in a 360-degree view. It wasn't the prairie anymore. It looked more like a post-apocalyptic war zone with smoldering wrecks and cratered mud. Framing it all were the same mountains and moons. It was beautiful in the way abandoned buildings can be beautiful.

"I was thinking that we start slow and solo. In this mission, it's you against nine others in what we call a limited battle zone. You see that electrical fence over there? That will prevent you from leaving the zone alive. To give you a fighting chance, pardon the pun, I have patched you in through the Brazilian server. They're mostly newbies over there."

Thanks for the vote of confidence. I hadn't fired a single shot in Alphacore, yet somehow, I didn't like being labeled a newbie.

"So, you want me to kill nine Brazilian newbies with

freaking cutlery?" I said as I pressed the left mouse button and SoomoBrother slashed with the knife at nothing in particular.

"Not quite," Nick said as he leaned over me again, his cheek not more than five inches from mine, and pressed some of the number buttons on the keyboard. I was increasingly convinced of his obliviousness to the concept of personal space. Didn't he even see me as a woman and consider the potential ramifications of the closeness? Maybe all I was to him was a black-clad, asexual, basket case. "Press here to toggle between the different weapons. As you can see, apart from the cutlery, you have a shotgun and an AK47." Different weapons appeared in SoomoBrother's hands as I toggled in turn.

"That'll help. Now kiss these Brazilian bastards goodbye." I readied the AK47 and ducked in behind the nearest wreck. I felt my heart pump fear into my veins.

It was—I was—a disaster. What did I think, that I had some innate gaming ability that would suddenly make itself known to the world if I just wanted it enough? I was no better than the millions of idiots putting their stupid videos on YouTube or TikTok as they blow things up, or eat hot chilies, slab on makeup and hair products, or dance, expecting effortless stardom and wealth. What a racket that was.

In the first round, I was blown up by a grenade. In the second round, I was killed by sniper fire. In the third round, I was shot-gunned after no more than 30 seconds. So on and so forth. There was the eye-hand coordination thing that needed serious honing. I needed to be able to move and turn and aim, all in some magical symbiosis of the left and right hand, and of the left and right brain, all the while, maintaining a constant 360-degree awareness of my surroundings.

Finally, after at least a dozen tries, I got in my first kill. It was more luck than anything else. I rounded a cluster of dying trees, and there in front of me stood a warrior in red armor with his freaking back turned. He was a sitting duck. I aimed the AK47 right at his back, clenched my teeth, and set off a hail of bullets towards him. Enough of the flying chunks of burning metal hit him to drop him. A rush of giddy pride pulsed through me, blurring my focus for long enough to get me killed again. But no matter—I had done it. It was downhill from here.

"Not bad," I heard from behind me. "Not bad at all." Dead Brazilians littered the landscape before me. I had lost track of time again. I ripped off my headgear and shot out of the chair. Nick looked impressed for real.

"Gotta go," I said, avoiding eye contact, embarrassed again at my loss of control, a state compounded by the wet stains under my armpits. My armpits hadn't crossed my mind for weeks, is there a jungle there now?

"See you back soon?" Nick said mockingly.

"I don't know," I said, almost to myself as I made for the door. "I don't know."

I hadn't dared to hope, but my dad was in my dreams again that night. The wind in his hair, serenity on his face, under that same tree on the top of a hill, framed by the mountains and moons of Alphacore. I shouted, I waved, I jumped, I tried to run to him. I could never get closer.

The next day, after having taken a long shower and decimating the jungle under my arms, I sat in my window all afternoon, waiting for Nick to get home. At 6 pm, he still hadn't shown up. At 7 pm, his parents were home, but his room was dark. 8 pm... nothing. 8.30... nothing. 9.15... still nothing. Who the hell does this guy think he is, leaving me hanging like this? Some warning would have been nice.

Nick never got home that night, which meant that my sleep was different shades of black—dreamless. I had to repeatedly force my way back into consciousness, out of sleep, for fear of being trapped in the void. I awoke exhausted.

The next afternoon, Nick finally appeared in his window.

"Where the hell have you been?" I yelled as he pulled his

window open.

"Hello to you, too," he said.

"What do you have to say for yourself?"

"Your assumption that I have nothing better to do than to game, or help you game for that matter, is, frankly, a bit insulting."

"What did you do then? Tell me."

"What are you, my parole officer? I was at Jamaal's house."

"Doing what?"

"You know, hanging out," Nick said feebly while looking down for an instant.

"I knew it!"

"Knew what?"

"You were in Alphacore!"

Nick sighed. "Fine, we dabbled a bit in Alphacore. When you're done with your psychotic ranting, pop on over to get your fix."

I had started to play almost every day. Nick was mostly hands-off, literally and figuratively, but did prove useful when it came to imparting some of the subtler aspects of the game like crouching and multi-stepped jumping. But most of the progress was my doing. I noticed a growing fluidity in my gaming, coupled with improved spatial awareness and honed multitasking abilities. Soon, the Brazilians were no longer a match and I joined a good ol' American server.

The pattern was sustained. The nights I gamed, I saw Dad in my Alphacore dreams. The nights I didn't, I had to battle the void.

One evening, I was tapped on the shoulder again. "My mom was wondering," Nick said, fidgeting hesitantly, "if you'd like to join us for dinner."

I pulled off my headgear, "Me?"

"Yes, you. Who would have thought, right?"

"When?"

"Like, right now."

Why would they want to share their dinner with a street urchin? I hadn't been in a social setting for weeks, could I still use a knife and fork?

"I don't think so. I'll just stay up here. You go ahead."

"What if I said that *I* want you to join us?"

What is the worst that could happen? That they want to talk about me and my situation—that would come to no good. I might even do something impolite. The last thing I needed was their pity.

Before I knew what was happening, I heard myself saying, "Fine." I stood up from the gaming chair and held up my hands. "I just need to wash these." Nick pointed to one of the upstairs bathrooms.

In the harsh light of the bathroom mirror, I stared at myself... my pathetic little self. The darkness under my eyes was in stark contrast to the whiteness of my sun-starved skin, all framed by the stubble of my scalp. I looked like a child vampire.

I grabbed the sink as I felt my chest tighten, as if the sink could save me from a panic attack. Would I have to smile? Smiling was so foreign to me now. I splashed some cold water on my face and gave it a couple of good slaps. I tried a smile, it was there on my face, but you could tell it was fake from a mile away. It would have to do; it was all I could muster.

I realized that I didn't know Nick at all when we sat there at the dinner table. Nick's father took hold of my left hand, and his older sister, Abby, took my right hand in hers. Nick's dad's features were not as sharp as my dad's, but his hands felt eerily familiar. Abby had Nick's smile. The fact that they were probably hand-holding religious wackos suddenly didn't scare me much.

"May we be grateful for the food before us," Nick's father began, "and may we be grateful for the gentle roof over our heads." He paused. "Above all, we are grateful to have Lily at our table, in our home." I could feel Nick's father squeeze my left hand gently and Abby squeeze my right. "May we be present in this moment and think of those less fortunate than us—for the suffering is indeed boundless." My hands burned and my world tilted slightly on its axle.

I was an observer that night, allowed to sit on the bench and follow the wax and wane of conversation, the laughter, the honesty of it all. Every now and again, I caught Nick throwing a glance my way. Try as I may, I think I failed to prevent an errant smile from appearing on my face. I might even have laughed that night.

SPEED FREAK

I t was well into October. I'd been playing Alphacore nearly every day. I had ventured as far as Nick's house, with Nick as my own personal Miyagi, guiding me through the nerd-infested jungle of online gaming geek-o-rama. By now, it wasn't only the dreams of my dad that drove me, it was something else. Then, one afternoon, my doorbell rang. I wasn't in the habit of answering the front door anymore, but whoever was outside was making it clear that they weren't planning on going anywhere any time soon, and besides, it wasn't like they were interrupting anything.

I had grown weirdly accustomed to Nick and the smile that fit his face so well, but I had never invited him to my house, let alone my room. "Got something for you," Nick said with barely concealed excitement when I opened the door, motioning towards the big fat box in front of him. Sensing my hesitation, he continued, "But it's pretty heavy. I'll need to carry it up."

I didn't like this development at all. Letting someone in too close seemed fraught with risk, but I was somewhat intrigued. "Fine," I relented, pointing him upstairs.

"Wow, you really got a moon thing going," he commented as he took in my room. "You're not a werewolf or something, you know... like what's her face?"

"Leah Clearwater, funny."

The snow globe I had used to assault Nick wasn't the only moon-themed item in my room. I had moon wallpaper, a moon bedspread, moon slippers, and so on and so forth. A stranger could be forgiven for thinking I was a lunatic, or, at the very least, extremely childish.

"Open it," he said, pointing at the box he had set down on the lunar carpet on the floor in the middle of my room. I pulled open the top flaps and peered down into, plastic, metal, and wire.

"What is it?" I asked.

"It's for you. A new world."

Nick spent the next half an hour unboxing his creation and setting it up on my desk. Although not a full-blown computer geek yet, I could still tell that it was something special. He plugged it into the mains.

"You do the honors," he said, pointing to the computer frame on my desk and pulling out my chair. "Here, sit."

"Whatever," I said. I sat down and pressed what looked like a power button. The computer let out a low confident hum and came to life with florescent light escaping from behind its Plexiglas siding, where blue incandescent liquid circulated in transparent tubing, like some cybernetic alien.

"It's beautiful," I said honestly, "but why... I don't understand."

"It's yours. I built it for you."

"I can't accept it... it's too much... it must have cost..." My emotions surprised me as my vision blurred, slightly.

"You have no choice. I mean, you've made some improvements, but now that you're going to join JRN, you're gonna need to practice day and night."

"J-R what?"

"My team in Alphacore, Just Regular Noobs. We just lost one of our own to computer overdose and we need a new member, like yesterday."

"Yeah, right."

"You bet. We are going to this big tournament in a few weeks, and I've told the others that you might just be the key to our success."

"But—"

"Now that I've built you this water-cooled speed freak of a computer, the only one to blame if we fail to reach the final round is you. Besides, I can't have you hanging out in my room all the time, my parents probably think you're my girlfriend."

"We can't have that, can we," I said, turning my face away from him. I'd been having dinner at Nick's place for almost a week now. They didn't even ask anymore. My place between Nick's dad and Abby was set. Every evening, I held their hands. After that first dinner, Nick had explained to me that it wasn't a religious thing, more just about practicing gratitude. He said his parents were card-carrying humanists. I wasn't quite sure what a humanist was.

"Anyhow... now that you have your own rig, it's time to build your own character," Nick said as he pulled up an extra chair to mine. "And you're gonna have to find a better chair, you need elbow support," Nick explained.

"Can't I just use SoomoBrother? I've gotten used to him."

"Nope. Living and dying with your own character will give you a sense of accomplishment at a whole other level. It's like you never really love anybody else's kid as much as you love your own, no matter how cute that other kid is. Your kid is just special. Its slobber is special. Its fecal matter is special." And almost to himself, he said, "Explains why my parents would ever think you could be my girlfriend..."

I must've played at least 80 hours of Alphacore in total. I never felt, or at least not since he died, as alive as I did when battling it out in the other world. "Sure, I'm ready."

"Just a sec," Nick said suddenly, then disappeared downstairs. He came back half a minute later with a blanket-covered rectangle and placed it on my desk. "It's one of my old ones, so you'll have to upgrade at some point," he said, pulling off the blanket to reveal a monitor. "But it will do for now."

He plugged the monitor into the rig, and the Alphacore logo was already alive and well on the screen. "I found a used copy on Ebay," he explained, "and it's loaded with a six-month subscription to Alphacore's dedicated network."

He placed a headset over my ears and lowered the see-through visor over my eyes.

One of the things that sets Alphacore apart from its competitors is, at least according to Nick, that characters are almost endlessly customizable, within certain set parameters, of course. It's apparently even possible to import your own artwork. It took us a while, I wasn't the best decision-maker, but after an hour, we had finished building her.

"So, for the final, and most important touch," Nick said triumphantly, "you're going to have to name your baby."

For a brief moment, I considered choosing a male character. I had, after all, been playing male for the past weeks and it felt shamefully empowering. But when I thought of the dearth of women in the gaming world, and the chauvinistic portrayal of female characters when they do appear, it would have been a betrayal of my gender. "I think I'll call her Luna," I said as I contemplated my creation.

Luna had long pigtails, a t-shirt, ripped jeans, and bright red sneakers. On her head, she wore an old-school leather football helmet, and most importantly, she carried some very big guns. Her eyes were bigger than mine, but she had some of my freckles. She was a version of me, and it was time to take her on a test run.

My love for Luna was instantaneous. I suddenly understood what Nick was talking about, what it means to play your own character. So, I started out slow, instinctively wanting to keep her out of harm's way, I kept her out of the battle zones—for now. I continued my ongoing exploration of Alphacore. The forests, lakes, prairies. I knew that Luna was governed by the same laws of physics that the Alphacore programmers had developed for all the millions of characters roaming this virtual world, but somehow, when I put her through the ropes, asked her to run, jump, crouch, climb, and swim, she seemed faster and better than SoomoBrother.

My bladder brought me back to real life. I flipped up my

visor, took off the headset, and turned around. Nick had gone. It was almost 1 am. Nick must have snuck out, who knows how long ago. Alphacore had such a voracious appetite for time, like congressmen for campaign contributions, it was frightening. I walked over to the window, the only blueish light there was came from the moon. Nick's room was dark.

That night, I was in Alphacore again, but my dream was more intense and the colors more vivid than ever. My dad was under his tree. He had that same subtle contemplative expression on his face and that same wind in his hair. I still couldn't get to him, but this time, when I shouted to him, I could swear that I saw him move his head slightly in my direction, as if he thought he heard something but wasn't entirely sure.

Nick's gift would let me visit my dad every night. Nick could never fathom his generosity. It overwhelmed me. How could I ever repay him?

THE NOOBS

I n the last week of October, I was officially inducted into Just Regular Noobs at my first ever LAN-party in Nick's basement. When Nick told Jamaal and George that he had a candidate for the open spot on the team, they were skeptical. They were probably looking for a seasoned player that could get them to the final round, so they essentially demanded a try-out.

"It's no big deal," Nick said, trying to calm me down as he broke the news. "Just show them what you got."

"You guys should be happy anybody wants to join your lame outfit."

Nick smiled, "Chill, Lil, they're just nerds being nerds. To them, Alphacore is dead serious."

"Chill, Lil, yourself."

"You're definitively ready to join JRN. I mean, just look at how upset you get when your skill is being questioned."

So, we met for a try-out, pitting me and Nick against Jamaal and George in a series of battles.

"Mom, I'm going to a college frat keg party. Don't expect me home before dawn," I said on my way out the door with my dad's office chair, having already made several trips with my computer gear. "I'll just grab a handful of oxy from your jar here on the counter, oh and I'm out of condoms, but I'm sure the frat house has plenty lying around."

I could have said whatever, she probably wasn't even listening. I didn't see much of her. She was cooped up in her room most of the time, rarely even getting out of her bathrobe. She was a pathetic sight to behold. I rolled my gaming chair out the door.

In Nick's basement, I had just made the final adjustments to my rig and booted up Speed Freak, when George and Jamaal came down the stairs. One of them saw me first and stopped dead in his tracks, the other crashed right into him, and they both nearly tumbled down the stairs with half their gear. Only by awkwardly clutching the banister, and each other, did they avoid certain death on Nick's tiled basement floor.

They tried to gather themselves and managed to put down their gear on their assigned desks. "RBN is finally entering the 21st century with a female member," Nick grinned. "This is Georgios Ballas, aka George, aka Girth," Nick said. "What you would call a hard-core gamer, perhaps the best with a Heckler and Koch A5, and he also comes in handy as a meat shield. He's even a pretty good hacker."

"Hi," I said, stretching out my hand towards George. He looked like a caricature of a gamer with his pasty complexion, pubertal face fuzz, and considerable heft from too much soda and stasis, which would explain his handle.

"We've been in the same class since 7th grade, Lily," George countered.

"Oh, God... I'm sorry... of course... George!" I couldn't stop myself from blushing.

"George has, in fact, had a crush on you since said 7th grade," Nick added.

"Who hasn't? I'm Jamaal," Jamaal said, stretching out his hand. "We've only been in the same grade for a year or so. So, perfectly understandable that you wouldn't know who I am." Jamaal had a buzz cut and sharp features.

"Jamaal, aka Jarno, is a kick-ass sniper. He has stacks of head-shot records," Nick explained, clearly amused by the whole situation. My blushing continued unabated. "Let's get this show on the road. Why don't you two get your rigs set up? Lil and I will go get some forage." He took my arm and guided me towards the stairs.

"It's OK, worlds are intersecting," Nick tried as he gathered Dorito bags and Bawls in the kitchen. "It's a good thing."

"It is not OK... it is horrible and unforgivable."

"What the f, Lil! You were supposed to cover me. What's going on?" Nick said next to me, while George and Jamaal sat directly opposite, facing us behind their monitors. We had lost the first two rounds—badly—and it was my fault.

That introduction earlier had jarred me, I couldn't shake my sense of guilt. I was stuck in the real world and couldn't let myself immerse into Alphacore's soothing digital embrace. I shut my eyes and tried to go back to a different time, on the water, skimming across the waves with my dad laughing and shouting by my side. The boat's hull smattering against the chop as we flew together across the bay. The smell of salt and musty seaweed singed my nostrils and made my synapsis sparkle. They took this from him. They took this from me.

"Lil," I opened my eyes to see a worried Nick glancing over at me. "It's time for the next round, do you need a minute?"

"No, I'm good," I said, gritting my teeth. "Sorry about earlier." I let my anger transform me into what I needed to be—a vehicle of destruction. "Let's own these mothers."

We started killing it. Nick and I worked in harmony as Nuffian, in fatigues, combat boots, and a red bandana, and Luna, in her matching red sneakers, pigtails, and leather football helmet, danced through the crumbling cityscape that was our battlefield, making mince-meat of Girth and Jarno, one headshot, one critical hit at a time. Girth looked a lot like a darker version of Chewbacca, with black fur and a bullet strap. Jarno was a battle-ready Samurai, with a helmet, mask, ornate chest armor, and skirt.

"Two for two," George grunted as he took off his headset and wiped his forehead with the back of his hand. "I don't know what just happened, but it must be my keyboard, the keys are sticky, I must have spilled some Jolt on them or something."

"Nick, man, your shitty connection is just lagging up my play," Jamaal tried. "Honestly, I don't know how you live with yourself. You need a serious upgrade"

Nick grinned, shaking his head, "Last round. You acorn heads ready?"

My brain crackled and a sense of euphoria radiated out from the pit of my stomach all the way to my fingertips. As these fingertips delivered unholy vengeance on Girth and Jarno, I felt something I hadn't felt in a long time. It wasn't happiness, no, but a reminder of its possibility.

It was all over now. "Well, well, well, just looking at your pathetic sweaty selves, it seems pretty clear that we have a verdict," Nick said, pushing back his headset and turning to me. "Welcome to the team!"

I grabbed his stretched-out hand and we had a celebratory shake. In my state of euphoria, I thought for a second that a hug would be appropriate.

George and Jamaal were in shock, hardly expecting to be crushed by a girl, let alone a totally stuck-up newbie like me. They tried to suck it up. "Yeah, welcome to the team," George said, sending me a nod.

"Glad to have you," Jamaal tried.

THE GOOD RAID

T ristan glanced over at Maria seated on the sideboard opposite him as she fastened a badge to her jacket and adjusted her baseball cap, both with the letters F-B-I on
them. Maria was one of the few people he actually liked at his
new gig—that baseball cap didn't make him like her any less.

Over the com radio, they heard, "Two minutes and count-
ing."

"Copy that," Frank replied. Frank was no more than 25
years old, yet he had a full grizzly bear of a beard. The bureau
had been forced to relax facial hair rules in order to recruit the
younger set—a nice Magnum PI duster, maybe, but this was ridiculous. "This better not be a PTA bake sale we're busting up,
Casco," the bearded one continued.

"Speak for yourself, I wouldn't mind some homemade rice
crispy treats just about now," Maria retorted.

They fell silent. Tristan held his Glock with both hands
pointed down between his legs and pulled the slide to chamber a round. He leaned his head back and closed his eyes and
breathed. Then, from the radio, "It's a go, go, go!" The van
lurched and he grabbed onto the strap as the van screeched
around a corner and slid to a halt. The door pushed open and
the team spilled out onto the Chinatown sidewalk just outside
Kung Paos Chicken Delight. With them were a couple of ICE
agents, but they held back.

Guns drawn, Tristan, Maria, and Frank rushed past the
relatively unperturbed restaurant customers seated in their

booths, wolfing down the all-you-can-eat buffet. They headed straight for the backdoor and out into an alleyway. Tristan could see rows of caged chickens lining one wall—hardly up to code.

They stopped at a nondescript door on the other side of the alleyway. It was locked. Tristan placed a couple of charges on the hinges and another one by the lock.

"Couldn't we just knock?" Frank asked, the geek inside him talking.

"This is a no-knock warrant. Take cover," Tristan said as he pushed the firing pin, and the door blew off its hinges, hit the wall behind them, and clattered to the ground. He rushed through the door, Glock in hand, and yelled, "FBI, everybody down, everybody down!"

"Nobody move, you are safe now!" Maria yelled as she ran in after Tristan.

"Jesus," Frank said as they took in the scene before them. Some bare lightbulbs dotted the ceiling, not providing much light or comfort. The main floor was packed with what must be at least 50 computer stations in several rows, all up and running.

"Police! Down on the floor! On the floor! Now!" Maria ordered as dozens of emaciated hollow-eyed faces turned from their screens. Some continued to work away at their computers as if in a trance.

In the far corner, Tristan spotted an elevated glass-enclosed control booth. Inside the booth stood an Asian guy with a tattoo on his neck, a cigarette in his mouth, and a smirk on his face.

Tristan pointed his Glock towards the booth and yelled, "Hands in the air!" The guy ignored him and reached for something on his desk. Tristan fired three shots into the booth, sending glass flying as the walls collapsed. Now the guy raised his hands with the smirk conveniently wiped off his face.

Maria lunged up the stairs to the booth, pushed the guy face-down on the desk, and cuffed him, "You have the right to remain silent."

Tristan holstered his Glock and scanned the room. Over in the far corner, steel-framed bunk beds lined one of the walls. As he approached, he saw some movement in one of the beds. Oh shit. "We need medics here!" he barked as he knelt down next to the bed. A young girl, who couldn't be much older than his own daughter, lay emaciated and barely responsive. He felt the girl's neck. "She's got a pulse, barely," he shouted. He took her hand, "It's all gonna be alright," he said softly, "it's gonna be alright."

This was the fourth Alphacore sweatshop they had busted this year. Indentured illegal immigrants, mostly from East and South-East Asia, were forced into slave-like conditions to play endless hours of Alphacore. The smugglers could then monetize the gains in Alphacore into real-life currency. But this was the first time they had come across misery on this scale, with an immigrant on the brink of death. Tristan could feel his jaw tighten. He thought of his daughter, Charlie.

As Maria came to the girl's side, Tristan stood up and saw how some cops led the tattooed guy out of the room and into the alley. Tristan ran, as best he could with his damned leg, after them. He caught up with them in the alleyway. "Wait up!" he shouted. "I can take him from here." The cops stopped, and with knowing glances, handed the guy to Tristan. Tristan grabbed the guy by the arm, the guy's hands still cuffed behind his back, and proceeded to lead him towards the restaurant's backdoor.

"So, you employ kids now?" Tristan growled.

"Hah, that one was too ugly to sell to the johns," the guy said with that damn smirk returning to his face.

Tristan grabbed the restaurant door as if to open it, but he didn't. He just kept walking the guy right towards the brick wall next to the door. A loud smack as the guy's face collided with the bricks. He groaned as the cracked nose released a tidal wave of blood.

"Christ, be careful," Tristan said calmly. He leaned in close, and in a near whisper, said, "Look who's too ugly for the johns now."

BROCCOLI

Moonlight tapped on my curtains. I thought of my dad, who used to tuck me in as a kid, and as we lay in my bed, we could often see the moon through my window. If the moon was out, I insisted on having the window open no matter what the outside temperature was. Dad took to calling me Luna, a roman moon goddess. "My Luna," he used to say.

My mom's door at the end of the hallway was closed as it was most of the time these days. I had a feeling that maybe I should go and knock on the door, see if she was alright, maybe step up and be the grown-up in the family. Instead, I chose the path of least resistance.

Sleep felt far away, with the adrenalin from the battles still coursing through me. I booted up the game, put on the headset, and flipped down the visor. My senses were immediately flooded by a digital tidal wave as the real world, with my mom in it, ebbed, and I entered Alphacore.

Now that I had my own rig, I saw less of Nick in real life, but more of him in Alphacore. Nick assured me that I had a standing dinner invitation, and I took him for his word, joining his family for dinner every so often.

Just Regular Noobs met up in Alphacore for nightly training sessions ahead of the biggest, I was assured, Alphacore tournament in the world. It was sweet, in a way, how seriously the guys took their training, I could not help but be drawn in. Next Saturday, the four of us would be heading to San Francisco with all our gear in tow—it was a Bring-Your-Own-Computer event.

We needed to practice, no time for distractions.

Nuffian and I were the first to spawn in.

"How are you?" he asked.

"Fine. Why?"

"Just checking."

Girth and Jarno spawned in and we stopped talking.

Without even bothering to say hello, Girth walked up to me and said, "Hit me."

"What?"

"Hit me!"

"Whatever," I said as I pulled out my 44 Magnum, pointed it at Girth's face, and pulled the trigger.

"Ahh!!" Girth yelled as his face contorted, "That was gnarly! I said hit me, not shoot me!"

"You didn't specify what you wanted me to hit you with," I said matter-of-factly. "So, I hit you with a bullet."

"What the hell is going on here!" our glorious team leader, Nuffian, interjected. "We need to stay mission-focused. We are supposed to be shooting at other people."

"I just unboxed and installed my new visor, the Shock Feedback 2.6," Girth explained, unable to conceal his excitement. "This means, ladies and gentlemen, that whenever I get hit here in Alphacore, I get juice zapped to my temples out there, in real life."

"Your parents are right," Jarno sighed. "You need to start thinking seriously about detox, after the tournament that is."

"I like to make things real, and it's adaptive, which means the more damage, the higher the voltage," Girth continued. "Don't you get it? It will make me a better player."

We were entering the battle zone and set to engage our next opponent, the team Demagogue42, in less than a minute.

"Knowing you, your strategy will backfire as you become addicted to yet another vice, pain, and go out of your way to get your fix," Jarno chuckled.

"What happens if you die?" I asked.

"Alright, enough doping around. Tournament is next

weekend. We have some tactics to work out." Nuffian took his role as de facto team leader seriously.

"Beyond fear!" Nuffian shouted as he rushed to engage the enemy.

"Beyond fear!" the rest of us shouted as we followed him with our battle cry.

I had found a new home in Alphacore, as crazy as it sounds. A home where I was in control and where guilt ebbed. I could spend all my nights fighting in the battle zones. The adrenalin, the constant focus on the now, the rush of battle, the near-instant feedback and gratification, it was like the best drug ever invented. But I started to notice that my brain had trouble coping with the constant input of the battles. I started to forget things in the real world and sometimes felt like I was on a large rudderless ship at sea, powerless against the rolling ocean swells.

Rather than cut back on Alphacore altogether, which would have meant spending more time in the real world than I wanted, and would have rendered my nights dreamless, I made sure to manage the time I spent battling. I was usually the first of the team to cut out for the night. At first, there was some grumbling, but as it became clear to all that the girl newbie had become the master, the most lethal killer on the team—not that the guys would ever admit it, their nerd pride being prohibitively strong—the complaining stopped. They could continue with their practice into the night without me.

I spent the hours before going to bed, or falling asleep with my face on the keyboard, exploring Alphacore. The world outside the battle zones and cities was so vast that much of it had to be built using algorithms. Not half the programmers in China could build it manually. I had found a place where the algorithms seemed to have stretched their own limits, the colors, sounds, shapes, and pixels began to take on life itself, and a godlike presence made itself known. It was in the corner of this virtual world that I first met Broccoli. Turns out we both shared lost souls.

That particular night, I left the guys to their battles and had just jumped off my vehicle, which happened to be a majestic white deer, Prancer, on the banks of a stream. Nick had, naturally, focused on battles and lethality when teaching me the Alphacore ropes. He had left out what must be the totally coolest thing about the whole damn game—you can ride the wildlife. I had discovered it purely by chance on one of my first outings with Luna.

Water in these parts behaved differently. I could sit for what felt like hours by a stream and watch the waters break apart to reveal hints of their mathematical origins. That day, I was lost in my own thoughts when I heard a rustling in the undergrowth not 30 feet from me. It was at times like these that I wish the game designers had allowed killing everywhere in Alphacore. As it was, weapons were only activated in battle zones. My trigger-finger was itching to light up the bushes, but there wasn't much I could do other than flee or wait for whatever was coming my way. I opted for the latter. I had nowhere else to be and nothing to lose. I didn't have to wait long.

"Seen any fish around here?" The voice came from behind me. I turned back around and on the other side of the stream, not more than 10 feet from me, stood a character right out of a Japanese cartoon. The pixels seemed to belong to another platform altogether. His colors were clearer, smoother, his eyes huge, his hair boyband fashionable, but fixed like a Donald.

"Fish?"

"Yeah, you know, if you put your hand in the water, you can sometimes catch one."

"Who the hell are you, and why are you following me?"

"Just a lost soul like you."

"That answers my first question, what about the second one? Are you a pervert or stalker or something?"

"I wouldn't call myself a pervert. I would chalk it up to happenstance."

"Happenstance? No one has used that word, and I mean

literally no one, since, like, before Jesus was born," I said, then stood up to leave. I hadn't traveled this far to talk to some damn stranger. If I wanted to do that, I would go to a real-life Starbucks or the bus stop near my house. "It's been a long day."

"I understand," he said, suddenly looking pathetic and forlorn where he stood on the other side of the stream. "You know, sometimes... sometimes I wonder..."

I whistled and my transportation came running, ready to whisk me away. I leaped onto Prancer and started off back towards the portal from where I came, about to leave the boy forever, but something made me stop. I turned the animal around to face him, "What?" I sighed.

"Which is the real life? The one here, or the one outside?"

"Uhh..."

"Sometimes I'm not so sure anymore, they blur, I hardly know..."

If there was one person in the whole world, both worlds, who should refrain from giving any sort of advice to anyone, it would be me. "Seriously, I really am messed-up tired. I need to go rest in the other world," I said, more softly now, "whether it is the real one or not." Hardly believing what was coming out of my own mouth, I continued, "I'll be back here same time tomorrow, other world time."

"Oh," he lifted his head and a faint smile appeared on his cartooned face.

"What's your name?" I asked as my deer carried me off.

"Broccoli... don't ask."

"I'm Luna."

FROM BEYOND THE GRAVE

From the comfort of my own bedroom, and with the computer Nick had made for me, I'd spent the past nights fighting battles alongside my new teammates. In many ways, it was just like any other sport—the more you practiced with the team, the more effective the team became. The team members find their place and build off each other's different strengths to form a cohesive deadly fighting machine. I still didn't have the manual dexterity and speed at the keyboard that the others had. What I did have, my singular strength, was my anger.

It was morning, not sure of which day. My mother's door was closed as usual. I lay on my bed not sure whether to start up my computer or not. Alphacore scared me. Alphacore was seeping into my brain. I dreamt Alphacore, and even when awake, flashes of Alphacore could overwhelm my synapses. Nick, George, and Jamaal were at school, of course, but I could join other teams for practice skirmishes.

I picked up the snow globe that I had thrown out the window just a few weeks ago. To think that I nearly destroyed the last thing my father ever gave me. I lay in bed holding it, feeling its heft. It would have killed Nick if I had hit him.

I looked at it again. Something caught my eye. In the middle of the globe, the full moon seemed to hover in its own inertia. As I shook the globe, and the stars swirled, a shadow I'd never seen before appeared to float inside the moon. The shadow was rectangular, as though a piece of Lego or something was floating in the semi-translucent fluorescent liquid inside the moon itself. I thought back to when dad had given me the globe, a few hours before he died. Maybe he wasn't giving me the globe, maybe he was giving me what was inside the globe. I stood up, too jittery to lie down. I didn't know what to do. I needed to talk to someone. Funnily enough, I didn't even think of knocking on my mom's door. The first person I thought of was Nick.

An hour later, when I thought he'd be home from school, I bowed to fate and rang Nick's doorbell. I needed a second opinion, and Nick was, despite everything, the path of least resistance. Nick's mom opened the door. "Oh, Lily, we missed you at dinner yesterday," she said. She had the crow's feet around her eyes of someone who smiled frequently, and for real. Without saying another word, she pulled me inside and gave me a warm hug. A hug that I hadn't known I needed. It felt good, and I didn't want it to end. Finally, she let me go. "Nick is in his room. You go on ahead upstairs."

I knocked on Nick's door but failed to get a response. I knocked again, nothing. I wasn't entirely comfortable walking in on a teenage boy. I had heard what they could spend hours doing to themselves and wanted desperately to avoid being a witness to it. I grabbed the door handle and carefully pushed the door open. I saw him before he saw me. He was bathed in the blue light of three screens. He was turned away from me and had the visor across his face and headphones over his ears. Both his hands were on top of the desk, thank you very much—the fingers of his left hand tapped away furiously at the keyboard, and the other hand was clicking on the mouse as he spoke commands into his mouthpiece. "Girth, take the alleyway to the east, and Jarno, you go up one flight and try to get a clear shot from the top floor." I was now not more than a foot away from him and he still had no idea.

"Any more headshots today?"

Nick shot out of his chair like a cat surprised by a cucumber and ripped off his headphones. "Jesus, Lily, you could have knocked!"

"Exactly," I said.

He caught himself and switched back towards the screen in time to see Nuffian blown to bits. He threw on his headphones, "You're on your own, guys! I've gotta go," and threw them off again, turned to me, and said triumphantly, "To what do I owe the honor of your visit?"

I pulled the snow globe out of the plastic bag I'd been carrying it in. "What, you're practicing without me now?" trying to pretend that my feelings were hurt, unsure if they actually were. I held the globe towards Nick, he flinched instinctively.

"Not that thing again! Are you going to accuse me of having broken it or something? I deny all wrongdoing. You probably broke it when you tried to kill me with it," he said, backing away. "You weren't booted up, so, since both Jarno and Girth still aren't up to par, I thought we might do a skirmish or two while we waited for you."

"Anyhow... look at it, the globe, look. Come closer," I said, holding it up to the light. "Just look at it. Do you see anything odd?"

Nick's face was mere inches away from mine. I could see his eyes through the globe. "That thing looks just as redundant as it did the last time I saw it. There are some small pieces of plastic floating around in what, by now, must be biologically hazardous water."

"Look inside the moon," I insisted, "take it."

"Huh..." he said as he rotated the globe in his hands, finally getting his thick brain in gear, "intriguing." He put the globe down on his desk and walked right out of the room. I heard him go down the stairs, and for what probably wasn't more than a minute, I was completely alone. Finally, I heard him come up the stairs.

"There's no way we're going to get whatever that is, out..." he said, standing in the doorway. He pulled out a heavy-duty hammer from behind his back, "Unless we smash it," and held it out to me. "You do the honors."

"No fucking way! It's the last thing he gave me!" I cried as I lunged for the globe on the desk and held it to my chest.

"Your father gave it to you? Don't you want to know? What if he intended for you to find whatever is inside?"

I looked at the snow globe again, with its wondrous swirl of stars. Smashing it would be smashing a tiny universe of love. But I couldn't deny that Nick had a point. What if it was something for me? Something my dad left for me. I realized that I didn't have a choice.

"Give me that," I sighed, signaling to the hammer in his hand. I placed the globe on Nick's desk. He was quick to move his keyboard and other computer-related paraphernalia. I gave the globe a tap with the hammer. Nothing. I tapped it again. Nothing.

"The thing didn't break when you threw it at me," Nick said helpfully. "Use some muscle already."

I raised the hammer higher this time and brought it down hard. The hammer clanged off the globe as the glass cracked and water started seeping out onto the desk. I tapped it again and the whole thing came apart, causing a miniature tsunami. The orphaned moon rolled onto the desk. Nick quickly soaked up the water with a towel. I picked up the moon and held it for the first time in my palm. The moon was made of smooth glass. There it was, the shadow in the moon, clearer than before. How the hell did my dad get something into it? I found no seams or evidence of tampering.

I put the moon back on Nick's desk. "Here goes nothing," I said as I tapped the moon carefully with the hammer. It broke and, again, liquid flowed out onto Nick's desk. I removed the shards and picked up the mystery rectangle—it was vacuum-packed in plastic.

"It's a memory stick," Nick said, looking at the thing between my fingers. "Looks like it's biometric."

"It's what?"

"It's a memory stick with a fingerprint scanner, so only

the right person, with the right finger, can access whatever's on the drive," Nick explained, suddenly grabbing the stick from me. "There's one simple way to find out if this was intended for you. I should have a USB around here," he continued as he rummaged through various piles of technology. "Here goes nothing." He pulled off the plastic from the stick, attached a cable to it, and pushed the other end of the cable into the USB slot of his laptop. He opened file manager and clicked on the icon for the stick. A window popped up.

This device is protected. Please place your left index finger on the device and pull down.

Nick held the stick towards me. I did as instructed.

Not recognized (9 attempts remaining)

I tried again.

Not recognized (8 attempts remaining)

"Maybe it wasn't for me, after all," I said, my heart sinking.

"Try it again, these things are finicky."

I tried again.

First layer unlocked.

"How the hell did he get my fingerprints?"

Second layer - ID verification

Please scan passport or ID-card using the built-in camera.

"That's lit! What line of work was your dad in anyway?"

"Back in a sec." I bolted out of Nick's room, down the stairs, and sprinted the distance to my house. I hadn't felt this light-footed in ages.

I grabbed my passport from my desk drawer. The last time I had used it was well over a year ago for a family trip to England to watch the America's Cup sailing race. Dad had managed to get me and him onto the Oracle boat for one of those rides usually reserved for sponsors and their families. The boat was 44 feet long with a mast over 80 feet high. It was multi-hulled and hydro-foiled. It was serious business. As the boat caught the wind, it heaved its mass out of the water, with only two tiny curved fins keeping it ocean-bound. My dad held me tight 15 feet above the water as we flew 40 mph. I clung to him as we laughed hysterically like we couldn't believe our own luck.

"Let's see if this gizmo is as cool as it sounds," Nick said as he held the thumb drive's camera above my passport and it emitted a pale blue light. Nothing happened for what felt like years, when suddenly...

Second layer unlocked

"Yes!" we cried in tandem.

Third layer - password protection

Please enter your password

"What! Must be some pretty heavy stuff on that thing," Nick said, "you know, like who killed Kennedy... or maybe even Kenny, for that matter."

I quickly typed in the password field.

Third layer unlocked

Access granted

Nick looked at me in awe. The folder in the finder window unveiled itself to us.

"Since my passport unlocked it, it must be for me, so it had to be a password that I could guess," I explained.

"Well?"

"I don't know if I should tell you. It's need-to-know only."

"You're kidding, right?"

"Fine, it was, L - U - N - A."

I clicked on the dedicated folder and it opened. Among the files on the drive was a video. I figured that it would be the logical thing to open it first, but I was scared shitless. It would have been nice to have Nick by my side when I opened it, but I really didn't know him well enough to cry on his shoulder or show any other vulnerability. He sensed this and said he was going downstairs to talk to his parents. When the door closed behind him, I sat down on his bed with his laptop on my knees. I placed the cursor over the video file, took a deep breath, and double-clicked.

The contents on the drive wasn't what I'd expected, if I was expecting anything. Maybe it was more about hope. It wasn't the last words of wisdom from a father to a daughter.

It wasn't like in the movies where they say something like: "*If you're seeing this, I have been murdered—and the murderer is... your uncle Marvin. He wanted the family business—you know, the almond farm—for himself.*" No, the video was grainy, shaky, badly lit footage of a meeting. What appeared to be four men... it's always men, isn't it? They were sitting around a low table, on a sofa and chairs. It was difficult to make out any details, but one thing was clear, my dad was not in the picture. I could only guess he was the one holding the camera. The sound was almost worse than the picture. Just muffled voices, some talking more than others, at one point what sounds like an argument, but with an unfamiliar cadence.

Apart from the video file, there were two other files. I could make no sense of them either. They both contained a bunch of seemingly random chains of numbers.

I heard a gentle knock and Nick's voice from behind the door. "You OK?"

I had no sense of how much time had passed. "It's fine, you may enter your own room now."

He scrutinized my face as he came back in, probably searching for traces of tears under the eyes or snot under the nose.

"I'm not so sure he left this for me. Maybe he put it in the globe just for safekeeping or something. He knew it was the last place anybody would ever look. He also knew that it would be safe, that I would guard it with my life, unaware of what it contained."

"Yeah, I mean, how could he have known that you would whip it out of your window in an attempt to kill your neighbor?"

"True."

"Well, what's in it?"

"Here," I said, turning the laptop over to Nick.

I thought that Nick, being a nerd and all, could help me figure out what the video contained. I was wrong. The video made little sense to him either. On the plus side, he did recognize one of the files on the drive, or rather a cluster of files. "Seems like you'll never have to set your foot in that damn school ever again, after all." Nick began to explain blockchain technology in detail. When he saw my eyes begin to wander, he stopped. Well, to make a short story even shorter, one of the files contained what seemed to be a motherlode of bitcoin, and that, at present exchange rates, I could live a gangsta life forever. "The fact that your father went to these lengths, covertly filming a meeting with a pinhole camera or something, putting a biometric thumb drive in a snow globe, is significant in and of itself." Nick closed the laptop. "The money is problematic."

I had never doubted for a second that my father was innocent of what they were accusing him of, and now the snow globe gave me something to prove it with. More importantly, it was a step in finding the bastards who did this to him—one step closer to wreaking unholy vengeance on them. We just needed some help in figuring out what we had. Nick, reading my mind, said, "I know a couple of guys".

"Jamaal and George?"

"George is, after all, a decent hacker, and Jamaal is not a complete idiot."

LEARNING TO FLY

"T wo incoming at 300 degrees!" Nuffian yelled. That same night we were at it again, honing our strategy and skills for the tournament. We'd finished off half a dozen teams with relative ease but were seriously pinned down by the Bloated Dragons. I was crouched next to Girth, behind a low-slung wall, while bullets and RPGs slammed into the wall or whooshed past our heads. I happened to glance over at him and regretted it immediately. I couldn't take my eyes off his Chewbacca nose, it seemed to have a life of its own, his left nostril, in particular. The nostril was pulsating. "Errr... Girth!" I said.

"What?"

"Get that finger out of your snout, will ya!" I yelled over the din of battle, and in an instant, Girth's left nostril returned to normal size.

In my headphones, I could hear the others chuckle. "You're such a dweeb. You keep on forgetting that you just spent 230 bucks on your visor," Jarno chimed in. "If you're gonna be data-mining your nose, you can't have the most accurate visor on the market."

"Fuck you both." Girth countered. "And Jarno, lucky for you they haven't developed a crotch visor yet."

It was time to end this battle. We'd been training for five hours straight and were getting tired and unfocused. My fearlessness, or to some, my recklessness, had become my calling card. One thing was for sure, it worked. I checked that my MP5 was fully loaded, turned to Girth, and said, "Now that you have both hands on your keyboard, think you can cover me?" I then jumped the wall without waiting for his response. I took several hits, but Nuffian, Girth, and Jarno all opened up with everything they had, and in less than a minute, the Bloated Dragons were history.

"Gotta go," I signed off, not even waiting for a response as I exited the battle zone. I mounted Prancer, who was waiting for me just outside the zone, and set out for the stream, not entirely sure what I was expecting or hoping for.

When I got to the stream, where the pixels were still doing their mathematical dance, there was no one there. It wasn't like it was a date or anything, far from it, but somehow, it hurt that he wasn't there waiting for me. That feeling of maybe needing someone scared me to the point where I was about to turn back to Prancer and leave this spot forever. Then I heard him.

"I didn't think you'd come," he was on the other side of the stream again, like he was shy. His cartoon eyes managed to convey a subtle melancholy, despite being painted with such broad strokes.

I walked up to the water's edge. "Neither did I," I said.

"What's really neat about this... our corner of Alphacore," he said as he produced what looked like a fishing rod from behind his back, "is that it is in constant flux." He hesitated as if waiting for a reaction. When none came, he continued, "The world is unpredictable, replete with randomness and on the cusp of deconstruction." As if on cue, a technicolored fish leaped out of the churning fractal water, and as it arced high between us, it seemed to merge with the air and reveal in flight the math from where it came. The creature caught the bate on the end of the fishing line and Broccoli pulled hard on the rod, whipping the line with such force that the fish burst into glittering pixels that rained down upon us.

Through the rain, his massive pupils fixated on me. "Makes you question what is real, doesn't it?"

"Things fall apart in all worlds, in all realities," I said.

It was the start of a friendship, I think. We would meet nearly every night after training. He didn't know me; I didn't know him. This made him mostly harmless, a risk-free bet. We had similar outlooks. The coolest thing about him? He had learned how to fly.

Broccoli whistled and, in the distance, I heard thumping. The ground shook, branches snapped, and a swirl of pixels could be seen rising from among the trees. Then it came crashing out of the brush mere feet from us and bounced up to Broccoli, wagging its tail like a dog. It was a two-story-tall kangaroo. "Meet Gilliad," he said as he grabbed the kangaroo's fur and swung up on its back. "Watch this," he said, beaming. He tickled the kangaroo behind the ears and the tail wagged faster and faster until the massive body started to slide across the ground. As they picked up speed, they began to heave into the air and the kangaroo tail rotated like the propeller of some freakish drone. Broccoli and his kangaroo were now airborne.

As they picked up speed and height, the kangaroo banked left and completed a circle 100 feet above me, then they turned and started to dive. It took me a second to realize that they were diving right at me. I reached for my MP5 before remembering that it was useless, and resolved instead to stand my ground. "You better not!" I shouted into my microphone, but no answer came. I wasn't about to let some Japanese cartoon and his giant kangaroo make a fool of me. The mass of fur was closing in on me fast, I could just barely make out Broccoli's grinning face behind the massive neck. I braced for impact, couldn't stop myself from squeezing my eyes shut, and whoosh, it buzzed by, mere inches from me. How I survived that twirling tail, I will never know. And then they landed, elegantly.

"Two questions, well... actually... three," I said as Broccoli came towards me with a wide grin. "What's wrong with you? How long have you known about this? When is it my turn?"

Broccoli explained that he discovered it as a fluke about two months ago, that it was probably some easter egg left by a programmer, which only works in this corner of Alphacore. "As soon as you try to fly beyond a certain invisible line, you basically disintegrate."

"Think I can do it with Prancer?"

"I've only ever flown a kangaroo, but I don't see why a deer wouldn't work."

I whistled, and a few seconds later, Prancer came strutting from behind some bushes. I grabbed him by the horns and swung up on to him.

"Now press R and T, and while holding those keys down, press the spacebar repeatedly."

I did as I was told, and on my screen, Luna tickled Prancer behind the ears and we slowly lifted from the ground. Prancer, being a deer and all, didn't have much of a tail to speak of, but the little he had rotated at high speed like one of them wind-up bunnies.

No longer a rookie gamer, I got the hang of it pretty quickly, and in a matter of minutes, Prancer and I were whipping through the sky doing rolls and triple loops. "That's whack! I didn't even know that was possible," I heard Broccoli shout in my headphones. I was already hyped, and his positive feedback didn't do much to mellow me out, so I pushed further. I pointed Prancer straight up and shot for the sky. How high could I go? "Uhh... Luna... where are you going?" I heard Broccoli in my headphones again. I didn't answer, I clicked off all communication and pushed further into the atmosphere.

As I looked down, I started to see the curvature of the planet, and off to the right, I could see the ocean stretch to the horizon. Clouds swirled around me. A flock of golden birds joined me in my flight, escorting me ever higher. The sky turned from baby blue to deep sky blue, to cobalt blue, to midnight blue as I approached the edge of space. Three moons loomed. Prancer's antlers and head and then his entire body beneath me began to dissipate, dissolve, and become nothing. I was all alone in space until I fused with eternity, and lost myself completely.

The fourth night we met by the same forsaken stream and took to the air. It was daytime in Alphacore, as it always seemed to be. We had dawn, dusk, and any shade of sky in between, but we never had night. Seems obvious, I guess, what's the point in having a game where you can't see where you're going, let alone who you're killing?

"I can't explain it," I said. "I just became everything and nothing, and then I woke up with my face on the keyboard."

"Now that's what I call a trip," Broccoli said, clearly impressed.

"Right up until his death, she was on his case, never letting up. Sometimes I can't help it. I can't help thinking, why him and not her? Why did he die and not her?" I said as I pulled Prancer up through a cloud.

"Not an entirely healthy thought," Broccoli said as he tried to follow me on his giant kangaroo.

"She was raging on him the day he died, you know."

"Do you ever really know anyone... even a parent?" When he realized he wasn't going to get a response from me, he continued. "Especially a parent. You think these fishes, this stream, these algorithms, are complex, right? On a scale from one to ten, I'd say the complexity here in Alphacore is a one. The complexity of your mother's mind is a ten."

"What kind of excuse is that?"

"It's no excuse. You wouldn't get very far pleading complexity in front of a judge and jury."

"Exactly."

"It's just a perspective."

"I'll show you perspective," I said, and without much thought, tilted Prancer hard to the right. No one had ever done this before, so I wasn't sure what was going to happen or how the algorithms would react. Prancer crashed hard into Gilliad's side.

"Whoa!" was the only sound Broccoli managed to utter before he fell. The crash threw him off and he fell hopelessly towards earth—or Alphacore's pixelated ground, to be precise.

"Oh shit!" I shouted.

"Thanks a lot… ahhh!" was all I heard in my headphones as he tumbled away from me at an alarming rate.

Come to think of it, I had no idea how gravity worked here in Alphacore, let alone aerodynamics. I was about to find out.

"Right behind you, bro!" I cried and forced Prancer into a deep dive. I could see Broccoli flailing below me. I was basically flying straight down and, evidently, going faster than terminal velocity because I was getting closer and closer. I was now close enough to see his face, and then just as Broccoli was about to hit the ground, I swooped in and grabbed him single-digit feet from death.

"That was totally crazy!" he cried as we dismounted. He turned to me, his pupils were, I hadn't thought it possible, even wider than before—like dinner plates. "Let's do it again."

MY SISTER, IO

We met up in Nick's basement the next afternoon. Nick had given George and Jamaal the latest info on the snow globe at school. They had immediately volunteered to help out. When they came down the basement steps, they looked at me with renewed respect and nodded knowingly as if to seal some sort of pact.

Nick placed his laptop on the coffee table and we plunked ourselves down onto the basement couch. I stuck the drive into the laptop and opened it up, going through all the same security layers as last time. I clicked on the video. The video was just as shitty as before. George was intrigued. He listened to one segment of the conversation over and over again until he leaned back. "I sure as hell don't know what these two are saying. But I can tell you one thing, it sure as hell ain't all in English."

"I agree. Based on the rhythm, I would say it was a Slavic language, leaning towards Russian," Jamaal added.

George clicked on the bitcoin folder. He paused for a second, looking like he was doing some mental math. He logged on to some bitcoin website.

Jamaal was following the computer screen over George's shoulder. "Holy shit!" Jamaal blurted out, "What kind of business was your dad into?!"

Nick punched him in the arm, hard.

"Environmental technology..." or at least that's what I'd always thought.

"It is a growth sector," George said in an attempt to disarm the situation. "Ordinarily, I would advise you to sell a chunk of coin to lessen your vulnerability to market fluctuations. But given your situation, we wouldn't want to expose you to any potential inflection points. "

"There is also the fact that the files on the drive are the only proof we have of the coins' existence," Jamaal added. "So, if something happens to the drive, you could get wiped out. What I suggest you do is make a copy, on another drive, and leave it here with Nick."

"Hah!" George scoffed. "I wouldn't trust Nick with my financial future, but you do what you have to do. When it comes to the Russians on that home movie of yours, I have an idea. I suggest we pay the Russians a visit, I know a white-hat... maybe gray-hat, hacker over there who might help us out."

For the bitcoin, Nick bought two extra drives for me the next day, and we made two copies. We hid one copy under the floorboards in Nick's attic, and the other was buried in my garden, in a vacuum-sealed storage bag inside a zinc container. We decided that the safe thing to do would be to delete the bitcoin on the original drive. Left on that drive, the one my dad had left for me, was the grainy video and a file none of us could figure out. I made a copy of these two files and placed them in an encrypted folder on Speed Freak.

Broccoli and I had been hanging out on and off for almost a week now. Talking, exploring, and flying. Other than meeting my dad in my dreams, it was, as little as I liked to admit it, the thing I most looked forward to in my pathetic little life. We were now almost one week away from the big tournament, and I was wandering in the meadow by the stream with Broccoli.

"Do you ever get out?" he said as he swung at the meadow with what was, absurdly enough, a golf club.

"What do you mean?" already not liking where this line of questioning was going.

"You know, out in the real world, with quotes around the real."

"You don't know the half of it." The time I spent battling solo, when the rest of the team was in school, and with the team in the evening and at night, coupled with the time I spent exploring and the time I spent hanging with Broccoli, a good chunk of the day was gone. If you add the time spent dreaming of Alphacore, there wasn't much time left for anything else.

"I've been out there, in the real world," he said and took another swipe at the meadow, flinging a plume of glowing pollen, pestles, and petals into the air around us. "It ain't so bad, you know."

He knew my dad was dead, maybe killed, he knew my mom was cracking, and he knew I was about to lose my house. How could he say it ain't so bad? I was about to tell him as much.

"There are rivers there. There are sunsets and sunrises there. There's the moon." He looked at me and smiled. "Admittedly, only one moon." In the sky above us, three moons hovered, and as I saw them, I thought of the earth moon, and the nights when my dad and I would stay up late to stargaze through the telescope he bought for me when I turned eight. The SF metropolitan area to the North threw light pollution into the sky, limiting what we could see. But we caught Jupiter and the rings of Saturn. If we were lucky, we could get a glimpse of the Orion nebula or Andromeda. We spent hours studying the moon in detail, her valleys and mountains, the Sea of Tranquility where man first set foot on her. My dad could tinker for hours every time we brought out the telescope, whistling tunes and talking to himself while experimenting with different combinations of filters and Barlow lenses, all to get the perfect setup for the conditions of that particular night. I rarely felt as close to him as I did in those moments. I could just sit and watch, absorb him, in need of nothing else.

I remember one clear, cool, and moonless night in late November, a few years back. The house and garden are in total darkness. Dad has even managed to get our nearest neighbors to turn off their own outdoor lighting. With a red flashlight in his mouth to guide him, he makes the last adjustments. I sit next to him on the back deck with one of his sweaters on me and a cup of hot cocoa between my hands. He is peering into the eyepiece and turning a dial, when finally, he says, "Wow..." He turns to me. "Check this out." Through the red light, I can see his eyes are glowing.

"Sure, Dad," I say as I put down my coco and approach the scope.

"Take a look," he guides me gently to the scope with his hand on my back. I bend down and rest my eye socket against the eyepiece. The gas giant, with its stripes and the great red spot, a storm three times the size of Earth hangs in my field of view. "Wow..." I say, without really understanding his excitement, we had seen Jupiter a half-dozen times already.

"Look closer."

Then, I spot her, tiny and yellow... Io. Oh, I'd seen Io, a Jupiter moon, before. She'd be hanging alone in the dark, to the side. But here she is, tracking across the surface of Jupiter with a new clarity. There is a second dot on Jupiter's surface, about the same size as Io, it's her shadow. Suddenly, I lose my foothold, my stomach sings, my brain fizzles, and I'm slung out into the solar system.

I'm now standing on Io, she has invited me, her volcanoes and molten lava all around me. The giant's gravity whips us together, across space and time.

I have no idea how much time had passed when I hear someone calling me back. I don't want to leave Io so soon, she is my sister... I want to hang on just a little longer, but I know I must go.

"Luna," I hear my dad's voice. "You there?" I look up from the eyepiece, earthbound once again. "It's called a transit," my dad says behind me. "That shadow is moving at 50 times the speed of sound across the surface."

Dad and I had often talked about packing our tent and sleeping bags and heading out to Death Valley and its Dark Sky Park. There, we could catch the Milky Way in all its glory. We will never be going to Death Valley, my dad and I.

70

Broccoli was looking at me inquisitively, studying me even. "Are you ok?"

"I'm fine... I miss him, that's all." I let my anger fade to sorrow.

BACK TO REALITY?

Not to brag or anything, but we'd been owning good since I joined the team. It was Sunday night and Just Regular Noobs were hunkered down behind some steel beam in what looked like a blown-out factory. We were just finishing off a weak team, ironically called OverForce, when Nuffian turned to me, still firing, "Luna, it's time now."

"Yeah, time to slay!" my Luna cried, opening up a fierce barrage of hellfire. "Let's finish these losers off!"

"No, I mean, it's time for you to go back."

I continued to pound the enemy position with all my fury. I knew what he meant, and I knew he was right.

"Time to get this over with," I cried and charged the enemy position, taking several hits as I crossed the space between us and lunged for the hapless warrior taking cover behind a low-slung wall. I sunk my combat knife into his back with a satisfying crunch, pulled it out, and crunched it into his neck, finishing him off. We had won.

"Fine," I said to Nuffian as I pulled out the knife. "But you'll have to cover me."

"I'll cover you, Lily... I'll cover you..."

The next morning, I stood in front of my open closet staring at the wardrobe of a stranger. What was I doing with so much to wear? It made me want to puke. I settled, instead, on a pair of standard jeans and a plain black t-shirt. My hair was basically still gone, a half-inch buzz covered my head, and I hadn't bought any more makeup since I threw out my old stuff.

Nick was waiting outside on the curb. As we set off on the walk to school, my backpack was light with a mere pencil case and calculator in it. I had no schoolbooks and no idea what schoolwork awaited me as a sophomore. I had missed the first two months. The night before, I had logged onto my school account for the first time since June. If I was going to school, it might be a good idea to know what my schedule looked like.

"Just remember, it's all about perspective," Nick said.

"What?"

"Nothing."

As we made our way to school, block by block, many of the streets quaintly sidewalk-less, it was as though I was rediscovering my own hometown. I had been out of school for weeks, but I had also been out of society. At first, cooped up in my own darkness, and then venturing out to the small circle of the team, and another world entirely. We passed familiar restaurants, shops, I think I might even have got some nods or waves of recognition. Restaurants and shops that I never again would visit with my dad. We passed *The Cricket*, where we'd celebrated his 40th birthday.

The closer we got to school, the tighter my chest became. We stopped a block away, where Ocean Street met Jefferson Avenue. Nick gave me a concerned glance and gently took hold of my arm. "You can do this. Just remember, 95 percent of people's thoughts are just incessant loops of self-obsession."

I let his hand guide me as we crossed the lanes of the avenue and stood, finally, in front of the school. He instinctively let go of my arm. I could feel eyes on me. Some of the kids probably thought I was some new kid, bussed in from the other side of the tracks.

Terrible things happen to people every single day, people ten times better than I am or ever will be. Just imagine the total amount of collective pain housed within the walls of this one school. You've got the perhaps tangible, like a brother with leukemia, a grandmother dying in agony, a beloved dog run over by a vegan food truck. Then you've got the more insidious kind of pain that can erode a life—the gnawing financial anxiety of a mortgage under water and a college fund depleted, the quiet desperation of failing and fading dreams, the haunting feeling of being forever disconnected from others, the hollowness of chronic depression, the shame of marital failure, the fear of loneliness, the forever wanting what others seemingly have.

So, why was I a novelty? Please just let me be embraced by our collective pain, let me bathe in our common sorrow.

As we made our way up the stairs to the main building, I glanced up at the morning moon hovering. The moon, caught between night and day, compelled, finally, to define itself in all its spherical glory—no longer a pancake, but an orb. My dad would have loved this moon.

We pushed through the door into the hallways and were met by a sea of familiar and unfamiliar faces, a sea that parted as we walked towards the lockers. Whispers, nods, careful smiles, a few confused looks. I was relieved to have Nick by my side and felt a compulsion to grab his arm, to lean in, but knew better. I glanced over at Nick, who walked upright with conscious authoritative steps like he was my bodyguard. Not to be a bitch or anything, but this must have been a highlight moment in his high-school career.

George and Jamaal, who were waiting for us by the drinking fountain, had wide grins on their faces as we approached. They couldn't believe their luck that they now had a girl in their little nerd clique, a popular—or at the least previously popular —girl, at that. My face flushed as I remembered when we met in Nick's basement and I thought it was for the first time. How easy it had been not to see, to filter reality like a real-life Facebook feed.

I bid farewell to the guys and set off to my first class, alone. I was still in a daze when I stepped into Ms. Dorsit's English class. "Oh, Lily!" she cried out in her high-strung British voice as she rushed from behind her desk to hug me. She held me by my shoulders as if to get a good look at me. "Why didn't you let us know you were coming!?" I didn't have anything to say, so

I smiled meekly and looked around the classroom trying to figure out what seat I could take. Reading me, Ms. Dorsit pointed to
a desk in the middle of the room. "Why don't you just take a seat
right there."

I plunked down behind the desk, feeling somewhat safer
there. I was staring at my own fingers when I sensed a sudden
change in the room. There, by the doorway, stood Sarah, knock-
down beautiful as ever, but tired and pissed. Without so much
as offering me a glance, she took a seat behind me and proceeded
for the rest of the class to burn a hole through my skull.

The English class was finally winding down, I think the
subject had been Chaucer—I could have picked a better day to
go back to school, but to be honest, I hadn't been listening
much anyhow. Feelings of guilt were welling up inside of me, ir-
rational as they had to be. I was the victim here after all, my dad
had died, right?

As soon as the bell rang, Sarah was out the door. I was just
about to run after her, or at least I like to think I was, when
Ms. Dorsit grabbed my arm. "Lily, dear, just a moment," she said.
"Principal Woods and Mrs. Rancetti would like to talk to you, to
welcome you back, my dear. Why don't you head down to the
office."

They were waiting for me in the office, ready to pounce. Principal Woods, with his closely cropped graying hair and sports
coat, looked the part and was mostly harmless. Mrs. Rancetti,
the guidance counselor, dressed in a flowery dress and thick
glasses covering half her face, on the other hand, was a pain in
the ass. She had expectations. She had hopes and dreams for her
students.

"Ah, Lily, I can't say how pleased we are to see you back
amongst us," Woods said sincerely, I think, as he pulled in three
chairs around one of the front desks. "Why don't we sit."

Rancetti closed the door behind me, muffling the sounds
of the high school hallway. "How are you, Lily?" She moved in
to give me an awkward hug before my body language persuaded

her otherwise. "I am so sorry for everything you have had to go through. I can't imagine..."

"Should I get a lawyer or something?"

"Hah!" Woods let out a forced laugh. He pulled out a chair, which I reluctantly sat down on. I had basically not spoken to anyone outside Alphacore for the past two months, and now, on my first day back, I was caught in a maelstrom of inter-human communication. I should have phased this thing in. "We thought it would be good to have a chat to set out a plan for the rest of the school year."

Rancetti took over. "First things first, how are you holding up? We have the school psychologist on standby if you need to talk to someone—"

"Competent?" I suggested.

"If you will, yes, someone competent," she continued, not taking the bate, "someone trained to talk to survivors of suicide in family settings."

My jaw tightened and my hands turned into fists. I wound up so tight that the words coming out of me had the volume squeezed out of them. "Let's get one thing straight, right off the bat... My father did not kill himself."

Rancetti and Woods looked at each other as if sharing a moment, like my denial was expected—typical behavior for a kid in my position. I wasn't having it. I stood up. "This conversation is over," I said, regaining my composure. I pushed in my chair and walked out, not giving them a chance to stop me.

THERE WILL BE BLOOD

My dad used to make the best sandwiches—whole rye, smoked turkey breast, rucola, mustard mayo. It was Tuesday, my second day back. I hadn't bothered to make any lunch, knowing full well that our fridge was devoid of any useful lunch components with the possible exception of the jar of mayo. George and Jamaal came to the rescue and let me pick from theirs—some carrot sticks from one and half a sandwich from the other. I didn't eat much nowadays anyhow, running mostly on fumes. In addition to the stubble on my head, the dark half-moons under my eyes, and my pale, almost translucent, skin, my cheekbones had been given a new prominence... a faint resemblance to some starved movie actress.

Jarno took a bite out of his sandwich, "You know, George here has a Twitch channel, he's been trying to build traffic for the past two years."

This was nerd-speak again, and it was passing way over my head. My failure to understand was compounded by my inattentiveness. On the far side of the lunchroom, Sarah, Carl, and Fenton were in their usual spots. My old seat was taken. It felt like an eternity since I sat at that end of the lunchroom. Sarah sat with her back to me, her golden hair swaying in animated conversation.

I turned back to Jamaal, "I didn't understand a single thing you just said."

Nick entered his mansplaining mode, his least attractive trait, but, admittedly, I had asked for it. "Twitch is similar to

YouTube, but specifically meant for streaming online games. The more people who watch your games, the more money you can make through subscriptions, ads, donations, and for the lucky ones, sponsorships."

"Anyhow, I checked your subscription numbers yesterday," Jamaal said.

"Good for you," George said, taking a sip from his red coke. I couldn't help thinking that he should switch to diet—he was a type 2 diabetes time bomb.

"How many subscribers do you think you have now, George?"

"I really don't know, Jamaal. It's not like I check every day."

"Would you be surprised to hear that it's 800?"

"I would indeed."

"In fact, yesterday evening, it was 814, to be precise."

"Wow, astonishing."

"Astonishing, indeed."

I hadn't talked to Sarah yet since returning to reality. I looked back over to the far end of the lunchroom. Fenton, balancing on his chair, couldn't help himself and made furtive glances my way. I avoided the glances as best I could, but I failed once and our eyes met. For a second, I felt like I was spiraling back to the party on the beach… to another time, another life, when I was my father's daughter. The invincibility, the hope, the sense of entitlement even, were all so foreign to me now, they had been obliterated. But Sarah, Carl, and Fenton were still on that beach. We were forever separated.

Jamaal's gibberish came back into focus. "Funnily enough, the correlation coefficient between Lily here," Jamaal indicated me with his open hand, should anyone be confused as to which one of us was Lily, "joining the team and the surge in subscribership of your Twitch channel, is perilously close to one."

While George was fumbling for a response, Nick intervened to explain again. "People are joining George's channel in droves, not to watch George, no, they are joining to watch you."

"What?!" I said, startled out of my near-coma.

"It seems that your totally reckless, death wish, kamikaze style is popular nowadays," Jamaal said. "What it also means is that the 800 times 2.5 dollars that George will rake in this month will have to be split between the four of us."

"What the hell!" George protested, pieces of baloney and tomato spurting out of his mouth. "It's my channel!"

"To think of all the gear I could get for 500 a month," Nick said, staring off into space.

"I'm not as stupid as I look," I said calmly. "It seems pretty clear to me, boys, that you're trying to screw me over. If I'm the main draw of the channel, the star so to speak, it stands to reason that I should be apportioned a majority of the revenue."

George glanced at a fictitious watch on his wrist, "Wow, time flies." He stood up. "We gotta cruise."

Nick and Jamaal followed suit. "See you after class," Jamaal said, grabbing his lunch detritus off the table.

"You don't look stupid," Nick mumbled almost to himself as he pushed in his chair.

I was suddenly alone at the table. The lunch crowd was thinning out. When will I ever feel like a part of all this again and stop being an outsider looking in? Over at the other side of the room, my old table stood empty. Sarah, Fenton, and Carl were gone.

I was in my first gym class since I got back. The whole thing just felt totally surreal and pointless. I used to be a starter on both the school volleyball and field hockey teams, in addition to my sailing. The gym used to be my element.

The team sat on a bench, the four of us in our shorts and t-shirts, waiting for Mr. Rockford to get the show rolling. I'd been allowed to borrow a kit from lost and found. My legs stuck out of the oversized shorts like ivory chopsticks. I looked down at my sorry limbs and realized that they hadn't seen the business end of a razor for months. Dark hairs lay stark against the pale skin of my shins—not many, and not thick ones, but it wasn't a pretty sight. I pulled up my socks as high as they would go, surprised that I cared, and could only hope that they would go unnoticed. I became acutely aware that Sarah, Carl, and Fenton were a mere two benches to my left. A coincidence that all seven of us were in the same class. A coincidence that I did not relish.

"George, hadn't your parents implemented a forced Wi-Fi vasectomy?" Nick asked as we continued to wait. "Don't get me wrong, we're thrilled and all that you're still with us, but—"

"He's hooked up to the neighbor's Wi-Fi," Jamaal explained.

"A felony? Great start to your new life," Nick said.

George held up his hands in resignation—his parents had sent him off to gamer rehab this past spring to try to wean him off his gaming addiction. The success of the rehab was mixed, to say the least.

For a second, Nick's bare arm brushed against mine and goosebumps rushed along my arms and up into my scalp. I was so not used to anyone touching me that I would probably have had the same reaction if I'd been touched by a dead skunk, at least that's what I told myself. As if he sensed something, he leaned in. "How are you?" he asked.

"Fine, why?"

"It's just, you know, finding that stuff in that globe of yours, we haven't really talked about—"

"And you chose *now* to talk about it?"

"Concerned citizen, that's all."

"Yeah, right," said George as he stood up and stretched awkwardly. "Whatever happened to upholding the eighth amendment?" George grumbled to no one in particular as he lumbered onto the gym floor. My teammates had never been much for regular sports in general and PE in particular. The system of picking teams in PE based on popularity seemed wholly archaic and cruel. In egalitarian, enlightened, socialist some would say, Sweden, the PE teachers were instructed to pick teams at random, and collective punishment was illegal.

The dodge ball swooshed past me, mere inches from my ear. Sarah didn't let up, her anger still palpable as she tried to mow me down. Fenton, on the other hand, seemed to deliberately avoid even noticing me, focusing his ire or disappointment on George, Nick, and Jamaal instead—with a particular inexplicable vehemence reserved for poor Nick.

I wouldn't be letting them go silently into the night, and did what I could to keep the barbarians from the gate. That didn't stop us from getting hammered. I heard a smack next to me and one of us went down.

"I see blood! Blood I tell you!" George cried as he sat on the gym floor holding his nose. George was being somewhat over-dramatic—there was a minute amount of blood, nowhere near Game of Thrones or Macbeth quantities. Nick stormed over to the other side of the court and put his face inches from Fenton's, "You're a real ass! It's just a damn game!"

"Back off, dweeb!" Fenton said, shoving Nick with both hands.

"Make me!" Nick said as he retook his in-your-face position.

This was infantile, but fearing it would come to blows, I inserted myself between the two, one hand on each chest, "Knock it off, you nutsacks." Magically, the two parted, both visibly uncomfortable.

"Alright, enough drama for one day, hit the showers!" Mr. Rockford shouted. Fenton, as if coming out of a trance, turned and walked out of the gym. Sarah and Carl followed him.

What the hell was happening? Why were worlds colliding?

"Sorry about that," I said, looking at George still on the floor, holding his nose, and at Nick who was standing next to him, still trembling with rage.

"You shouldn't apologize for that sob," Nick said.

I felt light-headed, almost like I was listing, like a ship taking on water. I took a deep breath. "We need to focus on the operation that lies ahead," I said, trying to redirect their attention. "We need to focus on Russia."

PERMAFROST

At first, George suggested sending the thumb drive contents ahead to his Russian hacker contact. This wasn't something I was ready to do. How could I trust anybody nowadays, let alone a hacker... a Russian hacker at that? George then offered to transfer the contents to a virtual thumb drive that Luna could carry with her into Alphacore. We decided to hedge our bets and only bring the video with us. Luna had the virtual thumb drive securely on her belt and could project its contents on any appropriate object.

George managed to patch us into the Russian Alphacore using something called obfuscated servers—way over my head —but it was supposed to make us untraceable. The Russian authorities had an even stronger need to control the flow of information than the Americans. We spawned in together into Alphacore Russia, all from our four separate bedrooms.

Jarno, ever knowledgeable, explained, "The Russians not only need to protect themselves from external and internal threats, but they also need to prop up a regime that is rotten to its core. These are the most corrupt bastards on the face of the planet."

Girth continued, "Yeah, we're now entering the realm of the same bastards that blew up several apartment blocks in Russian cities in the 90s, killing more than 200 people. 200 of their own citizens."

Jarno filled in, "I know, to create an excuse to start the second Chechen war. But let's not forget the Gulf of Tonkin when—"

"Jesus! Will you all stop nerding out? We shouldn't be hanging out here in this shithole country any longer than we have to. State actors are probably already looking for us," Nuffian said. "Ok, let's roll... beyond fear!" he cried.

"Beyond fear!"

In theory, there really shouldn't be a difference in the game rendering in the different Alphacore geographic zones, yet somehow, the difference was palpable as we spawned into Russian Alphacore. "Do you feel it?" I ventured as I pulled on a hoodie in real life.

"Yeah, I feel it alright. It's cold as hell," Nuffian said.

"Dreary is the word," Girth added. "Russia is the definition of dreary."

We tried to stay clear of the most populated grids and keep to backroads as we made our way from our portal toward the coordinates George had managed to get off his mysterious hacker contact—one he assured us was on the good side. We didn't quite feel like being drawn into any unnecessary battles, or questioned by any FSB agents. George had patched in a real-time voice translator just in case. Like that would fool anybody.

"This is it," Girth said.

"This is what?" I asked, looking around me. We were in the middle of a field with nothing but grass, trees, and cows surrounding us.

"We are where we're supposed to be, according to the co-ordinates."

"Get your weapons ready," Nuffian said as he scanned the horizon for incoming. "Seems like we've been duped."

"Seems like your white-hat hacker friend just turned black," Jarno looked through his scope.

"Let me check again, I must have gotten the coordinates wrong or something," Girth said apologetically.

"I say we retreat to the portal now before all hell breaks loose," Nuffian said, turning to go back the way we came.

"Wait, wait, wait," I said. I pointed to the nearest cow. "There's something seriously wrong with that one." The cow had what looked like a brass handle sticking out of its side.

"That's probably just so they can make milkshakes," Girth said.

"Who do you think you are, Shel Silverstein?" Jarno said, backing off. "Watch out, could be an IED,"

"An improvised explosive device," Nuffian explained.

"Thanks again for mansplaining the obvious to me," I said as I walked up to the cow and pulled the handle. The cow opened up to reveal a hatch.

"See, I told you we could trust the guy," Girth said triumphantly.

"Come on, get in the cow before anybody sees us," I said.

The hatch door shut behind us. The silence was total. We were standing at the edge of a huge chamber. "It's like Smaug's Lonely Mountain lair," Jamaal said, "just without the gold, the Arkenstone, the hobbits, the dwarves, the dragon, the vaulted ceilings, or even just plain rock for that matter." In fact, the chamber looked to be made entirely of brushed steel.

I looked back. The doorway we had just entered through was no more, only seamless steel. I glanced over at Nuffian next to me, he looked like he was thinking the same thing I was— we're trapped.

In the middle of all this gray steel stood a figure. The figure was either incredibly small, like a Lego, or very far away. It was impossible to gain any perspective in all the sameness.

"We have nothing to lose," I said and took a step towards the figure. Or, to be precise, I tried to take a step towards the figure. I couldn't move my feet. Nuffian, Girth, and Jarno were all also struggling against an invisible force that held their feet to the ground like with some giant magnet.

"Hey!" Nuffian yelled. "Let us go!"

Jarno raised his sniper rifle, put an eye to the scope, and put his finger on the trigger.

"Put the gun down," I said in a near whisper. "Something tells me this guy has a home-court advantage."

"Hey!" Nuffian tried again. "You know why we're here! No

need for all this crap!"

Nothing.

"The guy is obviously security conscious, to say the least," I said as I removed my Magnum from its holster and placed it on the ground in front of me. "Put all your weapons on the ground."

Girth, ever predictable, said, "I worked too hard for these to let some random Russian steal them."

"Just do as she says... what, you don't trust your own contact?" Nuffian said as he pulled off his own holster and dropped his AK47 on the ground.

Jarno reluctantly threw his arsenal on the ground, including a crossbow and the sniper rifle. Girth huffed and puffed like a little kid but finally placed the HKA5 at his feet.

My MP5 was now in front of me, I felt naked without her, as was my combat knife, and my Magnum.

My feet released and I could finally start the journey to the middle of the chamber.

Nuffian and Jarno were right behind me. Girth wasn't. He hadn't budged.

"You know what you have to do," Nuffian said without looking back. Girth grimaced as he pulled out a sword and, shaking his head, dropped it. He tried to move but his feet still wouldn't budge.

"We don't have all day," Jarno sighed.

Girth looked like he was about to cry, his lower lip quivered. For a second, I thought he'd rather stay put than give up his last weapon. With a great deal of effort, he brought out a gold-plated pistol and slowly placed it on the pile of weapons in front of him. His feet released.

It felt like forever. We walked towards the figure in the middle of all this sameness, and then walked some more, and then some more. At first, we couldn't even tell if the figure was getting any closer. But finally, I could start to make out some of the details.

"Who does he think he is, Ezio?" Jarno chuckled.

The others chuckled. I chuckled with them, having no

idea who this Ezio was—I learned later that he was some character out of a game called Assassin's Creed. Nuffian seems to have gotten the message and stopped his mansplaining, just when I needed some.

The figure was standing, facing us. He had a grayish cloak with a hood that threw his eyes into shadow. Only his nose and mouth were visible. After what felt like a mile, we stood face to face with him and I noticed that he was smoking. Ezio had a cigarette between his tight lips, the tip of which glowed in red. Two thoughts crossed my mind—is smoking conform with Alphacore policy, and what's the point? The ones and zeroes of Alphacore could carry with them kicks and addictions, just ask George, but it's not like they could deliver nicotine to the bloodstream.

Girth took the lead, "Greetings from the United States of America." No reaction. "Uhh... thanks for receiving us. Quite the setup you got here." I couldn't be sure, but it felt like he was looking straight at me, and it made me want to squirm. The silence was unbearable and Girth wasn't showing any leadership skills.

"He's not a fucking Martian," I hissed and turned to Ezio. "I'm Luna. I'm the reason we're here. I was told you could help me."

"Let's make one thing very clear," Ezio said finally, his voice cold like the chamber we were standing in. His eyes were pulsating red dots in the blackness under his hood—a real flair for the dramatic this guy. "We have no interest in helping you."

"But we were told—"

He lifted his right hand to say stop. "Our interest is to hurt, and eventually, destroy this regime. I think you might have information that could help us to do that."

"My interest," I said, trying to match him in his coldness, "is to find out what happened to my father."

"You see a problem where there is none. Our interests are inherently complementary. Helping you will be a byproduct of our efforts." He paused. Those red eyes pierced me. "I was told that you would be bringing with you something of value."

Instinctively, my hand felt for the virtual thumb drive, the only weapon left on my gun belt—a mistake. Ezio held out his left hand with his gloved fingers stretched out, at the same time, I felt the thumb drive vibrate under my hand, and suddenly, shoot through the air into his. Like Vader going after a lightsaber.

Nuffian, Jarno, and Girth all rushed Ezio while grabbing for weapons they no longer had. Ezio coolly held out his right hand and they were thrown backwards into the air, picking me up on their way, and we all came to a sliding stop on the steel floor.

Before we could protest and yell multiple expletives at him, Ezio waved goodbye, and with a smirk on his face, disappeared in a cloud of pixels. We were left dazed and alone in his chamber of steel.

"Thanks a lot, Girth," Jarno said.

"It's not like I knew that was going to happen," Girth said sheepishly.

I just shook my head in disbelief, my dreams of avenging my dad gone in a Russian pixel cloud. How could I have been so stupid?

"We'll find him," Nuffian tried.

Just as we were beginning to think that we might be stuck in this hell forever, the gray steel dissolved around us and turned to green, and we were again in the field where we had found that cow. Our weapons were in piles around us. A consolation for Girth maybe, but sure as hell not for me. We trudged back to our portal in silence and left Russia, vowing never to set foot there again. I was too disappointed to be angry.

THE WHISTLER

I t was Wednesday, my third day back at school, and I still hadn't said a word to Sarah. High school wasn't getting any easier, I didn't know if it ever would. I was a mess, with my dad, Alphacore, and the drive swirling in my head. Even the tournament was taking up a disproportionate amount of space in my brain. Being back in these hallways seemed both inconsequential and momentous. Whatever it was, I ended up spending an inordinate amount of time in the girls' bathroom—just to breathe. This is where it finally happened, where she finally spoke to me.

I pushed through doors to the bathroom, taking in its stillness. I took the second-to-last stall, theory and experience telling me that this would be the least used, and most likely to be tolerably clean. I pulled down my jeans, which came off easily nowadays. I sat down and relaxed, a stream of warmth left me and splashed timidly into the bowl.

"Lil?"

Startled out of my trance, I nearly jumped off the toilet seat while still peeing.

"I know it's you, Lil, I would recognize your pee anywhere," came from the stall right next to me.

"What!?"

"We've peed together so many times, I'd know that sound of yours anywhere."

"What!?"

"It's like a signature... a fingerprint. I just realized something, if you ever had a dog and you needed it to heal, but your lips had been ripped off by a Tasmanian devil, you could just crouch. You see, there is a slight whistling sound when you pee, and your dog would come running. Piece of cake."

Great, I whistle when I pee, another thing to worry about. I'd been running through my mind what I would say when I finally stood in front of her. All the words that I came up with, all the excuses, all the explanations, seemed so hollow. Now I was on a toilet seat, trying to think of a good comeback, and I was coming up empty.

"Uhh... Sarah..." the toilet in the stall next to me flushed. I waited for the sound to abate, it felt like the longest flush in history. "I'm sorry." Nothing. "I'm sorry I didn't ask for help... God knows I would have needed it... I still need it..." Nothing. She must be so mad, I had seen fury in her eyes when she tried to mow me down with dodge balls. I shut up and listened. Apart from the noise of the school hallway filtering through the door, there was silence. I stood up and pulled up my formally ass-hugging pants, then pushed open the stall door. The other stall doors stood open. She was gone. I was alone again.

DAMN FINE MULLET

Tristan was at his desk in the back of the NASA-like control room of the Cyber Gaming Unit. The job had many drawbacks, including a boss with a stick up his ass, a lack of upward mobility, lethargy, and young colleagues with facial hair, but one of the worst aspects were the working hours. Gamers were most active at night, so the CGU was at its most crowded between 9 pm and 3 am. Sure, most of the surveillance was done by algorithms and bots in close cooperation with Alphacore corporate's own intelligence gathering, which dwarfed the governments, by the way. But having boots on the ground was still operationally invaluable. It wasn't uncommon for the kids to take pot shots at law enforcement. He didn't engage, usually, despite an itch to blow everyone to pieces with his bureau-issued hyper weapons. The public relations department would not approve.

FBI leadership wanted the bureau to have a public presence in Alphacore. This amounted to opening up a "front office" in Alphacore's main commercial district. Getting Alphacore corporate to let up real estate required some behind the scenes strong-arming. A federal presence in Alphacore was not popular among the gamers either. The first iteration of the office lasted a day. At first, hackers tagged it with anarchistic graffiti until, finally, a particularly inventive one made it disappear altogether and replaced it with a three-story high fuming pile of pink elephant shit. Alphacore's programmers had begrudgingly rebuilt it, adding stronger protective layers and a few custom upgrades Tristan had requested.

The FBI office in Alphacore was set up with a tripwire so to speak. Any time someone entered the office, a notification was sent to Tristan's team. The team was then provided with a live feed from a virtual surveillance camera—all courtesy of Alphacore corporate. Without this setup, the team would have to constantly pull out on false alarms. Corporate did not give a damn if their platform was used as a tool to undermine democracy. They did, however, care a lot about the perceived threats of increased government regulation to their business model —ergo their willingness to accommodate federal law enforcement, to some extent.

Tristan spawned into Alphacore that night because the trip-wire had been set off, and the avatar that appeared in the office didn't immediately proceed to destroy it. Instead, there stood the ugliest mullet-bearing dwarf he had ever seen.

I was pacing back and forth in Nick's basement. "Why would you risk going to the fuzz at all?" George asked as he typed yet another unfathomable string of commands into his computer. Jamaal was doing the same on my computer. They had set up George's and my computer next to each other in some elaborate plan to mask my identity. Nick was hovering behind George, almost as nervous as I was.

"What else can I do?" I said. "We need help, and your Russian friend didn't exactly deliver."

"True," replied George, turning red at the memory of that debacle. "Back to the task at hand. The feds will train all their computing power, all those massive mainframes somewhere in a basement in Virginia, on you. To try to smoke you out, find out who you are and where you come from. You're entering the lion's den and we need to make you invisible."

"We won't be able to hold them for long. You need to be in and out within seven to eight minutes before your cover is blown," Jamaal explained as he powered up Alphacore on my computer.

"When we were in Russia, we used the relatively rudimentary obfuscated server trick. That won't be enough this time since we know that you'll be targeted and the feds have their head up Alphacore's ass," George explained. "There might be some collateral damage on the way, but the goal justifies the whatever," he sighed.

I replaced Jamaal in front of Speed Freak. "What do you mean collateral damage? Who is the collateral?" I slipped on my headphones and lowered the visor.

"No time to get into that now," Nick said, now hovering behind me as the Alphacore logo appeared on the screen. We had decided to take it easy with any Bitcoin spending, but the team had also collectively decided to make one exception for me, and that exception was staring me in the face. An ASUS Rog ultrawide 35-inch curved monitor, for two grand. It was nasty. The colors crackled. George couldn't take his hands off it, petting and talking to it like it was a Golden Retriever or something.

We had recond the FBI office the night before, so we knew which portal to use and how long it took to get from the portal to the office. "T-minus ten seconds," George said, suddenly serious. I put my hands in position on the keyboard and the mouse. "It's a go," I heard George now through my headphones.

I spawned into a side street a few blocks away from the feds, in Achore, the main city in Alphacore. I didn't like it here in the bustle of the city. I felt more at home in the outer rim, with my stream, and with Broccoli. Achore had the trappings of a modern megalopolis, with skyscrapers and pavement, noise and eccentricity, but it was not loved. It was like an unwanted bastard child—dirty, sad, and a pain in the ass.

We had chosen to use a completely new character, Roland, to try to minimize the risk of this all being traced back to me in real life. George had created a dwarf-like mullet-bearing creature. With George's help, I had patched in a voice modulator so that Roland would sound nothing like me when he spoke. I had a new virtual thumb drive on my belt... a replacement of the one stolen in Russia.

I passed a myriad of avatars on my short walk to the office. They all seemed occupied with their own lives, barely noticing me as I neared the office. I pushed open the front door of the fed office. On the inner door in front of me were instructions.

WEAPONS-FREE ZONE. PLACE ALL WEAPONS IN THE LOCKER TO YOUR LEFT. THE LOCKER CAN ONLY BE OPENED BY YOU. And in smaller letters underneath, it said: *The Federal Government takes no responsibility for lost or stolen property.*

I did as instructed. Roland didn't have much to lose anyhow in the form of valuable weaponry. I placed a handgun and a battle axe in the closet and closed the door. The inner door slid open automatically and I stepped in. The place looked like a cop station from an 80s TV show. Yes, I had seen some of the shows with my dad—Hill Street Blues being a notable favorite of ours. Metal desks were scattered around, together with dingy lighting and rotary phones, and phone books used to whack the perps in the head without leaving a trace.

Right in front of me was an unmanned reception. A small sign next to a big red button read: *Press For Agent.* Well, that's exactly what I did, and then I waited, and waited, and waited some more. No one ever said that the federal government was efficient. I needed to strike the right balance between keeping the rhetorical advantage and hurrying things along to get out within the time set for me by George.

"Yes," I heard someone say right behind me. I spun around. There, in front of me, stood an FBI agent, or at least what I suppose was an FBI agent. Of course, I could never really know for sure. He had a smirk on his face—this did not bode well.

"What, the federal government couldn't afford a decorator?" I said.

"As far as the decoration goes, it really is out of my hands. I kind of like the retro look though, thank you very much," the agent sighed. "Is there anything I can help you with? Got a crime to report or something? Maybe someone insulted your haircut?

Although, that's most likely not a federal crime. Had they insulted your height, then we might have had a case with the federal Americans with disabilities act and all."

"You've got a badge or something?" I said.

"I must have left it at home."

I don't know what got into me, but I went for him. I just went ahead and jumped him. I got two blows to his head. The rest was a blur. Somehow, the guy did a Keanu Reeves move and dodged my third punch with some karate voodoo. He got me in a classic cop chokehold.

"Christ, I think the polite thing to do would have been to introduce yourself before, you know, sucker-punching me," the agent said.

"Fine, fine, your place is the deal, you can let go of me now. I was just making sure you were legit. That move you pulled is not something they teach in your standard Alphacore classroom."

I heard George's voice in my headphones, "They are coming at us hard, you need to wrap this thing up."

The agent finally let me go and I could see his face again. He looked like the guy I had seen on some TV show my dad wanted me to watch from the last millennium, about two FBI agents hunting for aliens or something—was it Skulder or Mully?

"Okay, spit it out, what do you have to sell?"

"I don't want your shekels. I have information. I'm not sure you deserve it though."

"What you got?"

"I'll give you partial information. Prove to me that you've acted upon it, and I'll give you the rest," I said, trying my best to sound like I knew what the hell I was talking about. I had no idea where my moxy was coming from, I had, after all, been a paragon of meekness for the past months.

"You're hardly in a position to make demands," he scoffed.

"Forget it," I said, making as if I was about to turn towards the door. "I shouldn't have come."

"Fine, whatever. Shoot. What is your partial information?"

JRN had collectively decided to put onto the drive a copy of the file that contained the code neither of us could understand, but that was probably some sort of key. With one important modification, we removed digits in certain random places in order to render the code operationally useless. It was a crapshoot, for sure.

I unhooked the drive from my belt and placed it on the metal desk in front of me. "Enjoy," I said and started for the door.

"Wait! What is it? How can I reach you?" he asked.

"I'll be back here in 24 hours, you better have something for me then," I stepped towards the inner door and it slid open. I got out of on the sidewalk and breathed.

"No time to rest, you need to get to the portal now," I heard George's now frantic voice say. "They're closing in!"

I turned and started to run the three blocks to the portal. "Come on!" I heard Nick shout behind me. "You have 20 seconds." I slalomed between the avatars on the sidewalk, even knocking one of them over. But before they had time to react, Roland reached the portal and was out of there. My screen went blank. I ripped off my headset and looked up. Nick had pulled out the electrical cord powering the whole setup, effectively cutting off all communication.

BOYS WILL BE BOYS

Tristan flipped off his headset and leaned back in his chair, rubbing his eyes with his thumb and index finger—he still hadn't gotten used to all this screen time, which could give him splitting headaches. He turned to Maria next to him. "Got a sec?" he asked.

"Sure, boss, just let me switch to bot mode," she typed in some commands on her keyboard and rolled her chair over so they could see Tristan's screen.

He had already taken a look at the file the dwarf had left him. At first glance, it didn't make any sense to his non-geek eyes, but for some reason, he didn't dismiss the dwarf's information outright. The dwarf had, after all, gone to a lot of trouble to get the information into his hands.

He clicked on the file and the numbers—hundreds, if not thousands of them—tumbled out. Maria studied the stream of nonsense. "Looks like some sort of encryption key," she said. "I don't have the skills or hardware to squeeze anything useful out of it," she took her eyes off the screen and turned to Tristan. "Send it to Intelligence. They should be able to figure it out."

The recoil from the Glock pounded through Tristan's arm and into his upper body. It felt good. The rounds punched hole after hole in the target 50 feet from him. Underneath the main operations room, with its rows of computers and giant screens, someone had the foresight to dig out a shooting range. It was small, with only three shooting stalls, but that didn't matter.

Every now and again, he forced Maria and Frank to come down there with him in the hope that he'd make real agents out of them yet, but mostly, he was there alone. Tristan tried to get down there at least three or four times a week. It was better than any pills or talk therapy.

Tristan had just fired off his fifth 15-round magazine, the sweet smell of gunpowder lay thick, when the door to the range opened behind him. Richards peeked in his silly little head, with his silly little smirk on it. Supervisory Special Agent John Richards, head of the Cyber Gaming Unit, was Tristan's boss. Richards was fast-tracked right out of Stanford Graduate school, just as the FBI was creating CGU. Tristan guessed that part of that fast-tracking involved giving Richards pay on par with the private sector. In other words, multiples of his own pay, and the guy couldn't be much over 25. He was practically in diapers when the towers fell and the world changed.

Richards' mouth moved, but no words came out of it. He motioned towards a man who stepped in through the doorway, a man in a dark suit, closely cropped hair, and really shiny shoes. A man who looked like a caricature of an FBI agent of the Hoover mold. The only thing not quite right with the picture was the piece of gum churning in his mouth. Tristan glanced down at his own outfit. The vestiges of his former agent life were there—the tie, the dress shirt, and suit pants—but they were faded, wrinkled, and stained. He checked if he felt ashamed... he didn't.

Richards motioned towards his own ears and Tristan pulled up his earmuffs on one side. "This is agent Flip Maxwell, intelligence, West Coast office," Richards explained as they approached Tristan's stall. Richards was cautious as if Tristan could put a bullet between his eyes any second—not an entirely implausible scenario.

"That was quick," Tristan said as he put the Glock down on the stall table and turned to take the hand extended to him. Maxwell's grip was adequate, but his hand was cold and clammy. "We sent you the file like what," he checked his watch, "two hours ago?"

"You were in Helmand, right?" Maxwell motioned towards Tristan's leg.

"Yep," Tristan answered wearily.

"I like to know who I work with. I was just telling John, it's quite the operation you got here. I don't know why I'd never visited before."

"I have a few rounds left to fire off," Tristan nodded towards the range. "Wanna give it a spin?" He extended the muffs to Maxwell.

"Your hunch was correct, it is an encryption key," Maxwell explained as he grabbed the muffs from Tristan and pulled off his suit coat to reveal a crisp white shirt framed by a shoulder holster. "It was stolen a few weeks back."

"From?" Tristan asked.

Maxwell pulled out his weapon from the holster. Tristan could tell from the silver-colored slide that Maxwell was packing some serious lethality. "We know who the rightful owner is and they are eager to get the key back. It fits nicely in an ongoing investigation we're running." He stepped into the booth next to Tristan's and expertly pressed some buttons on the control panel to set up the target. He expelled the magazine and grabbed a monster 33-round magazine from the holster. He pushed it into the grip, the magazine extended a further 10 inches below the grip itself, it was that long.

"So..." Tristan tried.

"It's really on a need-to-know only basis. I'm confident that neither you, nor anyone at CGU, needs to know right now." He slipped on the muffs, effectively stopping the conversation dead in its tracks. He aimed, Tristan and Richards covered their ears, and he fired. The range exploded in a deafening rattle as 33 rounds hit the target in what felt like less than two seconds.

Is this guy for real? Tristan thought. What inherent insecurities would make him feel compelled to pack a military-grade automatic Glock 18 for a service weapon?

"It's me who needs to know," Maxwell said as he pulled off the muffs. He pressed a button on the panel and the target came sliding towards them. "I need you to tell me where the key comes from." The target came to a stop, or rather, half the target. It had been cut clean in half by the hail of bullets, leaving the bottom of the target on the floor.

"Intelligence seems to be a bit of a misnomer in this case," Tristan retorted, "if you think we will give you something for nothing."

"Now, now," Richards said, starting to sweat, half expecting them to start a gunfight then and there. "I'm sure we can find a way." Turning to Maxwell, he said, "Could you guys give us something to go on? It could make it easier for us to find something of value for you."

"The owner is a corporate entity," Maxwell sighed as he extracted the mega magazine and shoved in a standard-sized one. "The theft of the key is a theft of their intellectual property. The main suspect killed himself as we were closing in on him."

"So, all is well that ends well," Tristan said, getting increasingly irritated, not entirely sure why.

"Not really," Maxwell re-holstered. "You see, the key you found has been corrupted. It has been purposefully changed, just enough to be rendered useless. Whoever gave it to you has some ulterior motive."

"Blackmail," Richards volunteered.

"Could be..." Maxwell continued, "what we do know is that we need to find the person, or persons, who gave you the key."

"Tell him what you've got," Richards said, looking at Tristan.

"Christ, fine," Tristan stepped into his stall and picked up the pistol he had left on the stall table. "I'll tell you who gave it to me... it was... a dwarf. A dwarf in a damn fine mullet." He ejected the magazine and inserted a full one. "We don't know who gave it to us yet. We will be contacted again soon, and we should get more information then." He pressed a button on the command panel and readied a target. He wasn't in the habit of entering pissing contests, but he needed an outlet.

"Great, I want to be in on the meeting," Maxwell said.

"I don't think that's such a good idea. We'll record the interaction so you'll be able to see all that transpires after the fact," Tristan said as he grabbed a spare pair of muffs and slid them on. He saw Richards mouth something, but it didn't register, thankfully. For a second, he thought how great life could be if he just wore muffs all the time.

Tristan lifted his pistol and aimed at the target 50 feet away, his right hand steadied in his left. Then, he turned his head away from the target and fired seven rounds in rapid succession, then raised his gun slightly. "You're gonna have to give me more," he said, then fired another eight rounds, still not looking at the target. He lowered his gun and pressed a button on the command panel, and the target slid towards him. It stopped and it was clear to all that he had nailed it. A tight cluster of holes in the target's torso and another tight cluster in the middle of the target's head. An impressive display of accuracy and precision, he'd like to think.

Richards beamed. If Maxwell was impressed, he didn't show it.

SEND IN THE CLOWNS
- THEN KILL THEM

Tristan checked the time. It had been exactly 24 hours since they met the last time. He had already spawned into the FBI office in Alphacore, always surprised to see it still standing. He had no idea if the dwarf would show, but the reaction he had gotten from Maxwell led him to believe that the dwarf would. The system alerted him that someone was in the lock, and after a few seconds, the door slid open and there was the dwarf.

"You know that weapons are deactivated outside battle zones, right?" the dwarf asked.

"Correct."

"So, why all this ridiculous security?"

"Just a precaution and a way of filtering out the real crazies. Of course, you got in, so the system may need to be overhauled," Tristan said. "So, you gonna sucker-punch me now?"

The dwarf ignored the comment. "Last time we met, I gave you something valuable."

"Maybe... and you promised more."

"Conditionally, yes," the dwarf said.

"Information concerning the matter is classified as highly sensitive."

"Why?"

"The key you gave me belongs to someone else. It was obtained illegally, and just by possessing it, you're committing a felony."

"Tell me something I don't know."

"I'm going out on a limb here," said Tristan. "The key belongs to a company called EnviroTech. It unlocks files that are necessary to unlock a product that they have spent hundreds of millions of dollars developing. So, you understand."

"I'm going to leave now," the dwarf started to turn back towards the door.

"Go ahead and give it a try. I think you'll find the door locked."

"I might be a dwarf," the dwarf said calmly and turned back to face him.

"A dwarf with a mullet."

"With a mullet, granted, but I'm not stupid. You're stalling on purpose. Your in-house geeks are trying to smoke me out as we speak. Tell them to stand down. Tell them, or I will instruct my associates to destroy the key."

For a second, Tristan thought that maybe destroying the key would be the best for all. The blackmailers would have nothing to blackmail with, and Maxwell would fail. A win-win as far as Tristan was concerned.

"It worked!" George shouted next to me. I glanced towards him. "They're backing off," he tilted his screen towards me, the graphical rendering of our level of protection was going from red to somewhere between green and orange.

JRN were back in Nick's basement. "I don't like the smell of this at all." Nick was pacing nervously behind me. "Something's not right. I think we should cut our losses and abort now."

I cut the mic. "Don't worry, George is holding off the barbarians. Right, George?"

"I'm trying, I'm trying."

"Placing your life in George's hands, maybe not a strategy that I would deploy," Jamaal heckled unhelpfully from the couch.

I turned back to my massive beautifully-curved monitor. I had taken to calling her Marilyn. "Let's see where this narrative takes us." I hit the mic. "So, where were we?"

"You were just about to give me more information, and the uncorrupted key," Skulder answered.

"Yeah, right."

"Here, let me show you something." He waved his hand towards the far wall, and a hidden door hissed open.

"It's a trap!" came from behind me.

I ignored Nick and followed Skulder through the door. It hissed shut. Skulder waved his hand again, and the same door slid open and revealed another dingy 80s setting with gray paneling and bare lightbulbs. We stepped out into the room with one long bare wall with peeling paint. The wall to the right was lined with a row of lockers.

"Ok, what are we doing here?"

"Alphacore corporate are generally a pain in the ass to deal with, but they really outdid themselves when they built this thing... to my specifications, mind you." He waved that hand again and the wall disappeared. In its place stood a green meadow, backed by snow-clad mountains. "Or do you prefer forest?" he waved and the meadow pixelated into a forest. Sunlight slanted through the birch trees, refracting on the dew-covered grass.

"What does this have to do with anything?" I said, acting unimpressed. "You still haven't given me anything of value."

Skulder snapped his fingers—I didn't know you could snap your fingers in Alphacore—and a herd of white-tailed deer appeared among the trees. Their hooves scraped at the ground as they looked for something to munch on, and an occasional bird burst out in song. A fawn lifted its head and looked straight at me.

"This is lit and all, but could we get back to the matter at hand?"

Skulder did some other thing with his hands and the closets to my right all slid open at once. I tried to stay cool, but it was near impossible when there in front of me stood the mother of all gun lockers. Hanging in the racks were every kind of weapon imaginable, from standard pistols to rifles, to machine guns, to rocket launchers, to flame throwers. Many of the weapons I recognized, but several must be custom jobs.

"Go ahead," he said, pointing towards the guns. "Pick whichever one you want."

"The feds have a secret shooting range in Alphacore?" I said, walking down the row of weapons.

"I'm the only one that uses it," Skulder said.

I cut the mic and turned to George. "How are we doing?"

He turned his screen towards me once again. The dial was still in between green and orange.

"Careful," Nick said behind me. "He's getting personal. He's trying to lull you into a false sense of security. Make like you're friends."

I ignored Nick, again, as I tend to do when he frets. I hit the mic. "There has been at least one death associated with this case."

"I can't confirm or deny."

"I think it's common knowledge, it was all over the news. Anyhow, we have reason to believe that there was foul play involved."

"On what grounds?"

"I'll leave that for you to figure out." I picked out a SCAR-H rifle with an x-25 drum.

"Good choice. What's a kid like you doing getting involved in a mess like this anyways?"

"What makes you think I'm a kid?"

"It's just a hunch, that's all." He pulled out what looked like a modified M2, a belt-fed, tripod-mounted, monster of a machine gun.

"Big enough for you?" I said.

I followed him over to the range where the 80s room met the deer-filled forest. I thought of Prancer. "Do you think we could choose another target?"

"What?"

"I don't want to shoot deer."

"What then?"

I thought for a second, "What about clowns? I never liked clowns."

Skulder went quiet for a few seconds, probably whoever was controlling him in the real world needed to do some digging. Clowns don't exactly grow on trees. "Send in the clowns!" he said suddenly, and the forest came alive with Ronald McDonalds running around seemingly randomly, with their red hair and floppy shoes and face paint. They were truly frightening.

We opened fire at the same time. The forest filled with blast, dirt, wood splinter, falling trees, harrowing clown screeches, and above all, blood. Clown after clown was mowed down by our massive firepower. Skulder's M2 split clowns in half. Every single clown was slaughtered in a matter of seconds.

Skulder leaned his weapon against the wall. "Listen, I don't have a full picture either. You know how bureaucracies tend to work in silos... well, that goes for the FBI too. What I can tell you is that Westcap EnviroTech was working on nano drones that could be used to assist in pollination, to replace the bees being wiped out by colony collapse disorder. They could also be used for environmental cleanup, oil spills, and such."

"Why would anyone kill anyone over assisted pollination?"

"Exactly."

"You've given me shit all," I said. "It's time for me to leave." I dropped the gun and moved toward the door. "Remember, if you try to stop me or follow me, my associates will destroy the key."

Skulder shepherded me to the office, and then towards the main door. "What about..."

I turned around to face him one last time, I pulled a virtual drive off my belt and handed it to him. "Don't trust no one," I said. "Something doesn't add up."

I stepped out of the office, and once on the street outside,

I ran the whole way to the spawning point and got the hell out of Alphacore. Marilyn went dark, Speed Freak went silent. I looked up. Nick was dangling the power plug, again, in his hand. "You can't be too careful," he grinned. I understood why he did it, but every time he pulled the plug on Speed Freak, I felt violated.

The team had logged out from our latest foray into amateur sleuthing and was decompressing in Nick's basement. "I read something," Jamaal explained, "about it in Scientific American. We're talking about semi-autonomous military-grade Nano air vehicles, about the size of a mosquito."

"Sounds harmless enough," Nick said.

"Yeah, the only countermeasure you'd need is a military-grade mosquito trap," George said, ever helpful. "Bet they have them on Alibaba."

"There you're wrong, George. These drones, assuming they exist, would be AI-enabled."

"He means artificial intelligence," Nick interjected.

"Thanks, Nick," I said.

"So, they would avoid any trap you set. But that's not all," Jamaal continued, "these particular drones would also be able to make their own decisions within predefined parameters, and could work together using swarm technology."

"This just doesn't add up. My dad worked with an environmental technology company, he wasn't doing military stuff," I said. "In fact, he could go on rants about how the military industrial complex had infested our political life."

"That's the problem with dying," George said, this time not even looking up from his screen, "as your body is sunk into the ground, buried truths rise."

"Shut up, George," Nick said, slapping him on the back of the head.

"This is classic dual-use technology," Jamaal explained. "There's a civilian use, for example, cleaning up of oil spills like your FBI friend mentioned, but there is also a military use, for example, the pinpoint delivery of biochemical agents to kill enemy soldiers, or civilians for that matter."

"Your basic killer bees on steroids and PhDs. Nice," Nick said.

"But what was my dad doing in all this?" I wondered.

THE BAD RAID

T ristan didn't trust the clammy-handed, gum-chewing, intelligence agent. But his instincts, although historically flawed and even fatal, told him to stay close. So, he resolved to cooperate, but only as little as necessary. The FBI's own cyber forensics team had come up empty when it came to tracking down the dwarf. Tristan opted to keep Maxwell out of the loop when it came to the video the dwarf had given him. The only person he trusted with that information was Maria. He straight out lied and told Maxwell that the second meeting with the dwarf had been a wash, providing no new intel of value.

Instead, Tristan interacted with the not-so-helpful people at Alphacore corporate. They were so afraid of the whole privacy and personal integrity crapola, that getting information out of them by appealing to their common sense or love for country was like running into a brick wall. Tristan had to head down to the courthouse to get the only thing that could move them—a subpoena. Alphacore's sharks did what they could to throw wrenches into machinery of justice, but the judge didn't buy their spiel and swiftly struck down their appeal. Alphacore did, in the end, cough up the name and address of the dwarf.

Tristan shared the information with Maxwell on the condition that he be allowed to tag along to any intervention. That same night, he was in full tactical gear.

From what he could tell, they would be raiding an upper-middle-class home in a sleepy suburb. Their target was a 15-

year-old with no priors. Tristan couldn't help but feel that bringing in FBI Hostage Rescue Team, his former outfit and the most well-trained fighting force in FBI history, was a bit of an overkill. Maxwell had made the call.

Tristan slid onto one of the benches in the SWAT van and adjusted the Velcro on his tactical vest when he heard, "Casco!" He looked up and stared at himself, or rather, what could have been him if it all hadn't gone to hell.

"Josh!" Tristan exclaimed, forcing a smile. "What's it been..."

"Last time I saw you must have been, what, like two years ago? You were just shipping out. Damn, I was so pissed that I wasn't going with you, but no rookies allowed..." Josh must have grown six inches. His biceps bulged and his eyes had an alert intelligence about them. A perfect specimen of a man, in particular contrast to his own mangled body and soul. Tristan, to his own surprise, felt no hatred towards the guy. The van started moving. "Teaming up with the Deltas..." Josh shook his head as if remembering the good old days. The van went dark.

"That worked out just great, didn't it?" Tristan said, seeing now only Josh's outline as he chambered a round in his Glock.

"Some shit went down, for sure... for sure..." Josh trailed off. They sat in contemplative silence for what must have been quite a few minutes. Josh snapped back to reality. "Rolling in two minutes," he told his helmet-integrated mic.

"You know that our target is some 15-year-old, right?" Tristan said.

"We're aware of that. We've been ordered to use lethal force only as a last resort." Josh grabbed the handle and slid the van door open. On the sidewalk, Tristan could count a total of nine SWAT members, and Maxwell.

They'd parked the two vans around the corner from the target's house, and would make a stealth approach from there on foot. As they turned the corner, Tristan looked up at the house from the street. A blue light flickered from one of the upstairs bedrooms on the side of the house, the rest of the house was dark. The moonless night and autumn wind through the many trees along the street helped conceal their approach. Armed with Remington shotguns, M4 assault rifles, and Sig Sauers, the team single-filed along the side of the fence that ran along the right side of the front lawn. Josh took the lead, while Maxwell and Tristan, not official members of the SWAT team, brought up the rear.

When they were ten feet from the house, the team split up. Four of the men, carrying two carbon fiber ladders, continued straight towards the side of the house and stopped below the blue window. Three, including Josh, veered left towards the front door, while two continued around towards the back door. The ladder team swiftly but silently raised one ladder on each side of the window, and one man climbed up on each until they were level with the window.

"Ten seconds to breach," Tristan heard Josh's voice in his earpiece. Tristan had hung back so he could see both the side window and the front door. But when he saw that Maxwell had followed the front door team and had positioned himself ready to follow them in, Tristan unholstered his Glock and moved, as best he could with his damn leg, towards the front door. He wasn't about to let Maxwell out of his sight.

"M84, go!" he heard in his ear, followed by breaking glass as a flashbang grenade was thrown through the second-floor window. "Battering ram, go!" The front door imploded off its hinges as one of the men expertly swung the cylinder-shaped battering ram into it. A loud thud as the grenade exploded upstairs, and a shattering of glass and splintering of wood as the remainder of the upstairs window came crashing as they breached the room.

Tristan followed right behind the team as they ran through the front door and up the stairs. As Tristan approached the top of the stairs, he saw a body in a bathrobe face-down on the landing. An M4 aimed at the small of its back. He looked left and smoke curled out of one of the rooms nearest to him. He pushed past the men manning the doorway, realizing that he had lost sight of Maxwell. There, in the middle of the room, kneeling in glass and wood splinters, handcuffed with blood running out of his nose and ears, was the target. Maxwell triumphantly aimed his M4 at the target's head like he was taking credit for the raid's success—what an ass.

THE FIDGET SPINNER

Tristan's team's job was, in essence, to make sure that Alphacore didn't become a vehicle for organized crime to launder or transfer money, a tool for foreign powers intent on undermining our democracy or stealing secrets, or a channel for terrorist communication. It was needle-in-a-haystack work, so they relied on a number of informants to tip them off. These gamers were mostly in it for the money, their distrust of the feds was such that they rarely did it for their country.

Tristan docked into Alphacore. He scrolled through his avatar inventory—as an FBI agent, he had a multitude of options so that he could wander through Alphacore in disguise. Tristan chose one of his less politically correct avatars for this mission —an impossibly stunning female avatar called LakerGirl. She was dressed like a cheerleader, but instead of the pompoms, she carried two very big guns and a bullet belt strapped across her chest. The FBI avatar designers had gone to town with this one.

He spawned onto a forlorn trash-strewn, rat-filled city street in one of the seedier sectors of Alphacore. LakerGirl approached a rundown one-story building and knocked twice. A few seconds of silence and the door creaked open and Laker-Girl stepped into the Cantina scene from Star Wars. A heterogeneous mix of avatars were talking and exchanging items seated around tables and by the bar that stretched along one side. A few of the avatars glanced up as LakerGirl walked up to the table in the far back corner, where what must be one of the ugliest avatars in Alphacore, two tons of nasty complexion, sat alone with his back to the wall. Alone, except for two beefs who sat at the edge of the booth, their hands resting on guns on the table. They grudgingly moved aside.

"Rembrandt, do you mind?" LakerGirl said, grabbing the nearest chair without waiting for an answer.

"To what do I owe this displeasure?" Rembrandt puffed.

"I don't have time to go to someone else... you know, someone competent."

"Rush jobs are extra," Rembrandt continued, eyeing LakerGirl's special issue shotgun. He must know full well the weapons deactivation outside the battle zones didn't include those of federal agents and other law enforcement.

"On this," LakerGirl said as she handed over a virtual drive, "there's an AVI-file."

"You want me to write a five-thousand-word criticism of it?"

"I want you to look at it and tell me what you see. I want you to work on the audio and video to make it usable."

"Can't you do that in-house? Don't the feds like have the greatest crime lab in the history of mankind?"

"I want to keep this outside the house for now. How fast can you get it to me?"

"24 hours, if you beg."

The local news was running on the TV on the wall to his right when Tristan walked into the office. Richards sat behind a glass desk staring at the TV without acknowledging Tristan's presence.

The TV showed a kid being carried away on a stretcher, giving the thumbs-up and smiling as he was slid into the ambulance. The kid's angry mother was being interviewed on their suburban lawn. Scrolling along the bottom of the screen, it said: *Teenage gamer severely injured as FBI raid wrong house.* That summed it up pretty well. They had raided the wrong house. It hadn't taken long for an explanation to emerge. The IP address they had gotten off Alphacore corporate was the one connected to the previous owner of the account, which had been sold and transferred several weeks earlier. The kid they nearly killed was the previous owner. He had nothing to do with Maxwell's case. The whole thing was a disaster, and Tristan was about to take the fall for it.

"You're not in Afghanistan anymore," Richards finally said as he turned away from the TV and motioned for Tristan to come in. Richards picked up a fidget spinner from the desk and set it spinning in his right hand. Who uses fidget spinners anymore anyway?

"We were working on the information provided by Alphacore—"

"You were reckless, that's what you were. You can't go blowing up middle-class white kids on a hunch, and not expect political blowback." Richards seemed to have conveniently forgotten that Maxwell had made the decision to bring in the SWAT team. "When are you going to get that you're a dying breed? The days of the Riggs or the McClanes are over." He gave the spinner another spin and sighed. "Just keep your gun where your dick is, will ya."

"You mean up your—"

"In your pants, Casco, in your pants."

This was his second warning, the first one was for excessive force. A third time and a demotion or suspension without pay was coming his way. As if being stuck with the nerds at the CGU wasn't punishment enough.

He couldn't remember when things started to fall apart— was it before or after Amy left him? The custody battle was still raging. Ordinarily, he wouldn't give a shit about his job—his career was fried as it was. But no judge would let him see Charlie if he was both a recovering pill-popper and unemployed.

"The director is livid, and he's got the Attorney General breathing down his neck. She's looking for any reason to shut us down," Richards continued. Good riddance, Tristan thought but did not say—he was not one to shy away, but also not inclined to shoot himself in the foot for nothing. "The Alphacore folks are also pissed. Surprisingly enough, they don't appreciate it when we try to kill their customers."

"Christ, since when did we care what the Alphacore people think? No amount of money could buy the advertising they are getting from this thing." Tristan stood up to leave. "In fact, I wouldn't be surprised if they deliberately fed us wrong intel. They're a bunch of privacy rights hippies, after all."

"Enough excuses, next time you better get your information right, or you're out."

"Is that a threat or a promise?"

"I don't care if you're here out of some sort of misplaced gratitude for your service in Afghanistan," Richards said, fidget spinner spinning between his fingers. "We've all made sacrifices. You don't see me asking for handouts."

Could he fall much lower? Forced by circumstances of his own doing to stand there, silent, in the face of this mediocrity.

BYE-BYE STANFORD

I t was Thursday night. With only two days to go, we were, as per usual, faithfully practicing in the middle of the night. The curtains billowed slightly and the moonlight slivered into my room, competing meekly with the light from the screen in front of me. This was getting pathetic, the marginal benefit of further practice at this stage was approaching zero, or maybe in negative territory already. That's it.

"Hold it, guys," I said. The team came to a stop in the middle of a muddy field as the sun was setting in Alphacore.

"Uhhh, not the best of places unless you want a bullet to the carotid artery," Jarno said helpfully.

I placed a silver shoebox-sized device on the ground. "We're safe. Come over here and check this out."

"What is it?" Nuffian said, trying to act disinterested as the guys now stood in a circle around the silver box.

"An artifact, think we can sell it?" Girth suggested.

"Looks like a button on it, should I give it a push?" I asked.

"Go ahead, Luna, the honor is yours."

I placed my hand on the embossed square in the middle and pressed down. A white blinding light and a deafening thud, and all four of us were flung back, landing smoldering and twisted in Alphacore death.

"Cowabunga!" Girth grunted, "I knew I should have laid off the volt feedback loop tonight."

"What the… Did you just purposefully wipe out your entire team?" Nick cried.

"We have practiced enough. This is counterproductive," I explained. "We need a break, something that will fire up some complementary synapses."

"She has a point." Jamaal's and my emerging nerdiness were oddly symbiotic. "Many of our best athletes were omnivores while young, only specializing in their late teens."

"We're heading out into the real world tonight," I said. "Meet me outside George's in 20 minutes."

"You mean outside, outside?" George asked worriedly.

"You're lucky it's night, George, any sunlight and you would spontaneously combust," Nick laughed.

"Wear something warm, and something with a hood or baseball cap. Nick, can you get an Uber? I still don't have a cell." I switched off my monitor and glanced over at the wall where my cell had met its fate.

A little while later, we got into an Uber a block or so away from George's house. We rode in silence for less than ten minutes. The driver dropped us a couple of blocks from the main gates.

I hadn't visited the club since my dad died. We weren't members anymore. It was a bit past 2 am. The club was dark, the only lights were those along the docks, where multiple boats of various sizes bobbed in the night swell. Everything bathed in moonlight. I glanced up at the near-full moon that was high in the sky, as it is this time of year. It was approaching perigee, the point when the moon is closest to the earth, which explained why it was so huge. My dad would have loved this moon. He would have loved seeing it with me.

"Where the hell are we?" George asked as the taillights from the Uber disappeared around the corner. "I'm not feeling too good."

"It's all the oxygen. Your body is adjusting," Nick joked.

"You'll see," I answered.

"What's that smell. Rotten fish?" Jamaal asked.

"It's the sea, you noob," I said. "It's what life smells like."

The club contracted with a local security company that

did routine sweeps every so often during the night. I didn't see the company car and hoped for the best. I had basically grown up at the club and knew all its quirks, including a weak point. Just this past summer, a lifetime away, we—that is Carl, Sarah, Fenton, and I—snuck in a couple of times to go night-swimming in the pool.

I lowered my voice, "OK, guys, pipe down. Time to get rollin'." We began to walk along the fence toward the main gate.

Jamaal whispered, "This better not be illegal, Stanford doesn't like criminal records."

"Stanford doesn't like B-average students either, Jamaal," George chuckled.

"You can join me at the community," Nick added.

As we approached the gate, I pulled up my black hood and said, "Pull up your hoods or whatever, we've got CCTV up ahead."

"So much for Stanford," Jamaal said, barely audible.

We passed the gate and turned the corner to the backside of the club, where most members never set foot. We stopped in front of a trash compactor that lined the fence. "Here, give me a boost," I said.

Nick approached me and clumsily grabbed my waist. I let his hands linger ever so slightly before swatting them away. "Not like that, you dope. Here, stand with your back to it like this, and cup your hands like this in front of you." Facing him, I put my right foot in his cupped hands, then my left on his shoulder, and then finally hoisted myself up onto the compactor. The other guys followed. I could hear Nick groan under George's weight. We pulled Nick up last. The fence was a mere foot or so higher than the compactor, and on the other side, a very convenient tree grew. We used the tree to get down and were in.

I took the lead again as we snuck as best we could, trying to stay out of sight of cameras and guards. We approached the sailing school area, where I had spent so many weekends and summers.

"Here," I said as I grabbed four paddles from a stack near

the school office. "Anyone need one of these?" I held up a bright orange life vest.

George grabbed one, "I'll take one just in case."

"Are you kidding me? Even without one, you'll float like a cork. We could use you for a life raft," Jamaal said.

A half-dozen wooden steps led down to the dock. I stopped halfway and bent down. I felt with my hand under the third step. My hand closed around a glass jar.

"I found it!" I whisper-yelled as I held up the jar triumphantly.

"Found what, crunchy peanut butter?" Nick said.

"We are going for a ride," I said, shaking the jar, the noise of the rubber-coated key muted inside, "and I have the key."

The sailing school had a ridiculously overpowered Rib Craft with twin 150 HP Yamahas attached to the back. It topped 60 knots—which is fast for a boat—and we were taking it for a spin.

"My arm hurts, I think I might be bleeding from my armpit," George complained as we paddled the rib out of the floating dock harbor, two of us on each side.

"A few more feet," I said.

Jamaal stopped paddling. "I'm pretty sure this is a felony."

"Don't sweat it," Nick said. "Community college don't care, felony, misdemeanor, whatever."

We paddled in silence for another minute or so. "Enough." I dropped my paddle on the deck and got behind the helm. I flipped one power switch, and then the other. The twin Yamahas came to life with a guttural rumble, full of promise. I flipped on the automatic tilt and grabbed the wheel with my left hand and placed my right on the throttle.

"You'd better sit down," I said. The three of them obediently took seats behind me in the stern. I pushed the throttle forward an inch. Behind me, the engines engaged and let out a purr as the propellers churned the water and pushed us forward at a walking pace.

George barely had time to utter, "This wasn't so bad," when I yelled, "Beyond fear!" and slammed the throttle all the way. The roar obliterated the night and the boat heaved out of the water like a killer whale with a harpoon up its ass.

The moon guided us as we ripped a seam of white froth through the ocean. The lights of the city fading behind us. The wind whipped my hair and pulled the skin on my face back- wards like a cheap facelift.

I glanced back and met Nick's wide grin. He met mine and nodded. Jamaal looked like he was expecting us to breach the space-time continuum, and looking forward to it. George had his hands in the air and screamed in ecstatic joy. We had, finally, if only for a short while, moved beyond fear.

A little while later, I pulled back the throttle as we approached the club. Something was wrong. I could make out movement and flashlight beams dancing over the floating docks.

"We won't be needing the paddles this time. We won't fool anybody," I said and set course for the birth we had left an hour ago.

"Bye-bye Stanford, hello community!" George chuckled.

We had been lucky in our bad luck. A club member, probably kicked out of the marital bed, had been sleeping in one of the guestrooms above the clubhouse, and heard us when we set off. By some miracle, he called Sylvester, rather than security or the cops. It was Sylvester who stood at the birth when we docked and ordered us to follow him to his office.

"We called, you know," Sylvester, my former sail coach, said from behind his desk. "I came by your house, talked to your mother."

"I couldn't face anyone," I replied, my eyes fixated on the floor in front of me.

"This stunt you pulled today was dangerous. You put yourselves in jeopardy, and you put the school at risk." Sylvester was the head of the sailing school and looked the part. He had a chiseled weatherworn look with dark ocean-blue eyes, which I am pretty sure women might leave their families for.

"It was all my idea, sir. I basically coerced the others into following me," I tried.

"Don't sir me, Lily. I've known you since you were wee high," he said, holding his right hand not more than two feet off the ground. "I want you to know that I petitioned the club board to let you stay on at the sailing school, despite all that happened... said that you were an asset to US sailing, that you had Olympic potential."

"You didn't need to do that," I said, meeting his eyes.

"I failed. Some of the dinosaurs on the board were afraid of potential fallout, you know..."

"Because my father was a crook."

"I didn't say that—"

"Doesn't matter. So, when are the cops coming?"

"They're not," Sylvester said as he stood up from behind his desk and opened the door.

Jamaal suddenly perked up out of his daydream of a future as a permanent member of the bottom tenth percentile.

"What, no fuzz!" George blurted out.

Sylvester motioned us out of the room and the building, then, in silence, led us to the main gate. "You three," Sylvester said, pointing at the three boys, "I don't ever want to see you again." He opened the gate, motioned them out, and turned to me. "I'm so sorry you lost your father. Sam was my friend and I choose my friends carefully. He was one of the good ones." He put his hand on my shoulder. It could have been my dad's. "If there's anything I can do, let me know. Anything. Promise."

I nodded and followed the boys out to the world beyond.

Outside the gate, George was being ridiculous. "This was the best thing! The best thing ever!" he cried and flung himself over me with a hug. "Um, sorry," he blurted out, pulling away, face burning. "I didn't know it could feel like this. I mean IRL."

"You know what they say about near-death experience," Jamaal added, "well, they were right."

"I just ordered a car," Nick said, turning to me. "You alright?"

"I'm fine. It was amazing, wasn't it?"

"Yes, it was."

TWO GIRLS IN A SHOWER

Nick and I had walked to school together for the fifth time. It was Friday. He was actually humming, maybe lingering effects of the boat heist. Tomorrow, we were heading off to battle the hoards at the tournament. I'd survived almost a week at school. I'd like to say that it was getting easier every day, that I felt a belonging, but I wasn't convinced that the world of high school was any more real than Luna's world. My tribe, as far as I was concerned, was JRN. That's where I belonged, that's where I was useful, that's where I was assessed, not on who I was, but on what I did.

Weighing on all of us was the drive and its contents, and where it pointed. Although Skulder, or whatever that agent's name was, didn't say it in so many words, it was pretty clear that someone wanted that key bad, bad enough to kill. It could well be a suicide mission, but one way to find out who killed my dad was to flush them out. If they wanted it bad enough, they would come for me eventually... what then? I didn't have anything left to live for, so I was essentially risking nothing, but who was I to pull Nick, George, and Jamaal into it? I had no right to put them in danger. They were already exposed enough as it is, with their real and digital fingerprints all over this thing.

"Lil, your arguments seem rational enough," Nick said as he chugged back his single serving of milk at lunch. How cute, this wasn't the time to tell him that dairy was out, maybe even dangerous (although not as dangerous as Russians). "But you forget one crucial factor. George, you tell her."

George had just taken a massive bite out of his cheese dog and struggled to make himself intelligible. Jamaal stepped in. "What Joey Chestnut here is trying to say—"

"Joey Chestnut is the world record holder in hotdog eating," Nick interrupted. If he could just stop his mansplaining, he might even be attractive, to someone. "He downed 72 dogs in ten minutes, with buns mind you."

George, finally able to talk, chimed in, "They weren't cheese dogs though, just plain dogs, impressive nonetheless."

"Have you two finished?" Jamaal continued. "What Nick was trying to say is, the crucial factor you forgot is that we are a team. We cover for each other. We don't leave anyone behind. Not in Alphacore, not here."

"So, you're stuck with us," Nick said, suddenly serious. "We will go beyond fear, together."

It was all very melodramatic, but even a hardcore cynic like me couldn't help but be moved. There was an awkward silence. Luckily, we were saved by the bell. "So, I'll see you guys tonight for a skirmish or two?" I said. The vagaries of high school scheduling sent us on different paths for the rest of the day. My tongue stuck to the roof of my mouth, but there was nothing I could do about it. I had resolved to never again, for the rest of my life, pee in a public facility, which meant that I had to pace my liquid intake.

I made my way over to the science wing. Our chemistry teacher, Ms. Offerman, had been out sick earlier in the week, so this would be my first chemistry class since getting back. I was early. Having no idea what seating arrangements had been made during my lengthy absence, I chose the far corner of the lab. The class started to fill up, some of my classmates nodded in my direction, others even approached for small talk. But no one sat next to me.

Things settled down when Offerman came in and closed the door. She thumped down a pile of notebooks onto her table, then looked out over the class, her eyes landing on me. "Ah, Lily," she said, smiling, "I heard that you were back, I couldn't wait to see you." I blushed. "The day one of my best students returns is a good day!" Enough already.

"To continue our journey into metals," she proceeded with unabated enthusiasm, "we will today be observing—" there was a knock on the door. All attention was directed at the door as it was pushed open. In stepped Sarah.

"Sorry," she said as she closed the door behind her.

"Take a seat next to Lily in the back," Offerman pointed. "You must be thrilled to have your lab partner back." Sarah's facial expression did not seem to support this assertion. "So, metals and acids," Offerman continued, "you will need to exercise caution, put on your lab coats and safety glasses. Important not to cork the test tubes too hard, the cork goes on loosely, is that clear?"

Sarah plumped down on the stool next to me without even acknowledging my existence. Offerman's instructions faded into the background as blood thumped through my brain. I just did what everybody else did, went through the motions as we took out the test tubes, Bunsen burners, and prepped the acids. Finally, I couldn't take it anymore. "I never told you this before," I said as I dropped a piece of metal, I wasn't even sure which metal, into a test tube. "I wanted to spare you, but you were so honest with me in the bathroom yesterday... it's only right that you know." Sarah acted as if she didn't hear me, she added hydrochloric acid into three of the test tubes in the rack in front of us. So, I just kept on talking. "I'll just come out and say it. You snore. You're a snorer. My God you snore." Sarah rammed a cork in each of the three test tubes. "Why do you think I slept at your place so much more often than you ever slept at mine? My mom couldn't sleep with your snoring shaking the whole place. My dad even worried about foundational damage to the house."

Sarah sighed deeply, and finally turned to me and her eyes locked into mine through the safety goggles. This was the first time we really looked at each other since the party on the beach... before everything changed.

"You fart," she said, straight-faced.

"What?!"

"You're a farter, and I'm not even sure you realize it. You just go about your life leaking like some worn-out granny."

"That's it! You—" I wasn't sure I had an adequate comeback, but one of our test tubes chose this opportune moment to explode, so I never needed one. There was a loud pop and glass and test tube contents splattered across our desk. We just stood there paralyzed. Ms. Offerman rushed with uncanny speed over from the front of the room, grabbed us by the arms, and dragged us to the nearest corner. "Stand still," she ordered as she pulled a lever. We yelped in tandem as cold water poured down on us. I turned to look at Sarah, she looked at me, and we started to giggle, and that led to laughter, which led to hysterical laughter.

OFF TO THE RACES

R eality made itself known as pale light filtered through my blinds, announcing Saturday—game day. Considering the emotional rollercoaster I was still on, I was crazy to think I could handle 48 hours of, basically, non-stop gaming. But I had to do it for the team. I'd slept way too long. Jamaal's dad was swinging by in less than ten minutes to pick me up and drive the four of us to the tournament—a two-hour drive.

I slipped on our sponsor's t-shirt, a garish bright-blue thing with the wording "ClearView CarWash" on the front, and "JRN - Beyond Fear" on the back. Our corporate sponsor was the owner of a local chain of car washes, who just happened to also be Jamaal's father. In return for providing invaluable PR for his brand, we were given the ride to and from the tournament, and free caffeine-laced soda. Our team was punching way over its weight class, so looking like fools, I told myself, would be to our advantage because no one would see us coming until it was too late, when their bodies lay strewn all over the battlefield.

I looked at the thumb drive in my hand. It would have to come with me. I didn't dare leave it out of my sight. I made my way down to the kitchen. As usual, I was careful not to wake my mom. I tried to limit my interactions with her as much as possible.

Yet there, at the kitchen table, in her half-open bathrobe, hair in a mess, and with a mug of coffee in her hands, she was looking ten years older. It was too late to turn around, plus I wanted my tea. I said nothing as I turned my back to her, filled the electric kettle with cold water, and placed it on its stand. It started to hiss quietly. I popped a couple of slices in the toaster and pulled some milk and butter out of the fridge. I picked a butter knife out of the drawer as if a butter knife would be enough to cut the tension between us.

I hadn't told her anything about what I had found in the snow globe. She was in no condition to compute the information, plus she seemed so gullible, buying the FBI's story. Could I even trust her?

I buttered one of the pieces of toast and turned to face her. "Mom," I said with a gentleness that surprised me. Her eyes met mine and I saw her infinite sorrow. "I'm heading out for a few days. Are you going to be ok?"

"Have fun, darling," she answered, her tone flat. "I'll be fine."

"Do you even know where I'm going?"

"I trust you, honey."

"Maybe you shouldn't so much... trust me. There's a couple of pints of milk, some bread, and some microwave dinners," I said like I was the grown-up in the family.

A barely perceptible nod was all she could muster in acknowledgment.

I turned to butter my second slice of toast at the counter, but my appetite was lost. I saw the unbuttered toast start to crumple as my hand turned into a fist, and my toast was toast. Was it my anger, was it finally here? I wanted to turn and scream at her and ask why she had abandoned me. Ask how she could give up. Ask why she never smiled with her eyes. But I was saved by a honk. They were here.

I dropped the mangled bread on the counter and made for the back stairs to run up and grab the last of my stuff, but stopped in the doorway. I turned back around to face her. I hesitated for a second, but then asked, "What are we going to do?"

Her eyes met mine again. "I don't know," she said. "I don't know."

We were on our way. I was stuck in the middle between George and Nick in the back seat of Jamaal's dad's smallish Japanese car, happy in the knowledge that being a girl made me ineligible for titty-twisters. Given George's size, Nick and I were scrunched close together, with our shoulders, hips, thighs, and knees touching—not as uncomfortable as I thought it might be.

There was some traffic backed up to get into the parking lot, and a handful of parking attendants in bright yellow jackets were directing traffic as best they could.

We parked, and Jamaal ran out to get a couple of dollies from a row of them provided by the organizers. "BYOC does not mean bring your own chair," Nick said as George started to untie a chair that he had tied to the roof of the car.

"My ass's well-being is essential for JRN's success, I'm even thinking of insuring it. I have already reached out to Kardashian's people to find out what insurance company she uses," George replied as he struggled not to drop the chair or the red cap off his head. George had made an attempt at a costume—as I looked around the parking lot, I saw quite a few good ones.

"If you keep up your lifestyle, you'll need to check with those same people about boob insurance," Jamaal laughed.

"Is that all you could manage?" Nick said, feigning disgust as he looked George up and down. George had on a Mario mustache, red cap with an M on it, and blue overalls. The cap was too small, the mustache was off-center, and the overalls were so stretched out over his stomach, I thought he'd explode.

"Given all the crazy that's been going down the past few days, what do you expect?" George replied. "Your costume looks like shit too, by the way." Nick didn't have a costume.

Neither did Jamaal or I. To complement the carwash t-shirt, I wore standard jeans and sneakers—red sneakers this time, in Luna's honor. The only thing out of the ordinary was hidden from the naked eye, in the form of the thumb drive stuck in the condom pocket of my jeans.

We had brought so much gear that Jamaal's dad had borrowed a utility trailer to hitch to the car. We piled our equipment onto two dollies: a total of six monitors (George needed to bring three, of course), four keyboards, four overnight bags, including pillows, four gaming computers, four headsets, four visors, and lots of cables. Dozens if not hundreds of gamers were doing the same thing all around the parking lot. A majority of them were prepubescent, pubescent, and post-pubescent boys. Girls were surprisingly well represented though, as were men over 30. Men just don't seem to grow up anymore.

We had almost reached the main entrance when my heart twisted as I glanced to my left and saw bold letters splashed up on an adjacent building announcing that the *West Coast Annual Power and Sail* was opening its doors tomorrow. I used to go to the boat show with my dad.

"This way," Jamaal pointed, looking up from his floor plan as he led the team towards Hall A.

"Holy shit," Nick exclaimed as we entered the hall.

"This is huge," George said, all the while trying not to look too impressed. In front of us stretched row upon row of computers being set up. Two football fields totally covered in row upon row of battle stations. Thousands of computer screens lit up the hall like slot machines on a Vegas floor. The beamed ceiling was clustered with spotlights. At one end of the hall was a stage. Along one side was a raised and roped-off platform. Nick explained that this is where the ranked teams could hang out and wallow in swag—free Red Bull, donuts, so on and so forth, and not have to co-mingle with the plebes. A sign advised us that we were entering a Wi-Fi restricted and mobile data restricted area.

"To stop cheating," Nick explained. "Alphacore has built their own dedicated network just for this event."

"Alphacore are control freaks," Jamaal chimed in.

We checked out the seating chart again and headed for row A 32, more or less smack in the middle of the hall, and started to set up our gear at the table we had been assigned, which was now to become our battle station, at least until the final rounds. Nick and I were in the middle and Jamaal and George to our sides.

The star teams were automatically qualified for the round of 32 tomorrow, while the plebes, a group of which JRN were members, needed to duke it out in several qualifying rounds during the first day and night to snatch the 16 remaining spots. The stars mostly hung out in the VIP section meeting with sponsors, Tweeting, Snapchatting, YouTubing, Instagramming, or giving interviews to various news outlets.

Our first round was to start in a mere 30 minutes but I couldn't sit still, thoughts of my dad swirled. "I'll be back in time for the game, I promise," I said as I headed for the exhibitors in Hall B.

"What about our strategy session?" Nick shouted behind me, taking his team leader responsibilities a bit too seriously maybe. You mean the strategy where I blow everyone out of the water and lead us to victory? I wanted to say but didn't. That I, a two-month noob, could outgun the rest of JRN blindfolded was still a bit of a sore spot.

Hall B was a jungle. I looked around trying to get my bearings, seeing all sorts of gear and software companies, from the big ones to more obscure outfits that sold customized gear.

LET THE GAMES BEGIN

The crowds in Hall B were thinning as the gamers were heading back to their stations. I followed the crowd back to Hall A, many of my fellow gamers were carrying tote-bags stuffed with loot from companies trying to woo this growing and valuable market segment. I had barely made it back to Hall A when I heard, "WELCOME, GAMERS!" blared out from the main stage. The multicolored lights flared up and a gigantic screen lit up with a 20-foot-tall Alphacore logo projected in 3D. There was a space right in front of the stage where gamers were beginning to cram in like a nerd mosh pit. Not in the mood to rub myself against sweaty and under-deodorized teenage gamer boys, I continued to make my way back to my station.

"T-minus 30 minutes until you noobs get going with the qualifying round," the announcer continued, "but until then, please welcome our master of ceremonies for tonight, the one and only, the most famous YouTuber on the planet, Oz! Blondie!" The crowd surged forward as a diminutive figure in a standard t-shirt and jeans and a leather trench coat and boots with 20-inch soles, came swinging from the rafters. He landed on the stage and stood for a moment taking in the crowd.

"Welcome to the greatest tournament on earth!" Blondie continued into his headset as the crowd roared. "Your battles will be broadcast across the globe. The final, to be played in a little less than 48 hours, will reach 500 million people! A world record!"

"Yah! That's gonna be us, I tell ya!" George shouted as I returned to my station. He was ecstatic, totally in sync with the crowd in the nerd-pit.

"What are you on?" I countered.

"You'll see. It's all about mindset," George continued, undaunted.

"Then we're in trouble," Nick said. "One of us is not in the mindset."

"And that would be?" I tried. Silence. "Me?"

"Bingo," Nick said, still staring at his screen, not man enough to look me in the eyes.

"She'll come around," said Jamaal, "right?"

"Do we have a surprise for you!" Blondie shouted from the stage. "We have a new setup this year. We have 2500 teams battling it out in this qualifying tournament. Of those 2500 teams, only 128 teams will make it to the next round and have a chance to make it to the finals the day after tomorrow." The crowd roared again.

"We have an accelerated process this year. In 25 minutes, the battle will begin. And I mean battle in the singular." A less than enthusiastic applause from the crowd. "Instead of one on one battles, we will have the biggest deathmatch in history! A free-for-all massacre, the likes the world has never seen."

"What the..." George tried. Followed by scattered cries of surprise.

"At exactly four pm, we will start the clock. Teams will have exactly three minutes to get to wherever they think is a good spot. After these three minutes, your weapons will be activated, and the killing begins. No re-spawning, no second chances—if you're dead, you're dead. However, to make things interesting, we have tripled all your HPs. Remember, only the top 128 teams will go on to the next round."

"This is whack," Jamaal said, clearly stunned.

"See that giant ticker there?" Blondie said, pointing to the number "2500" up on the screen behind him. "When that reaches 128, then, and only then are you safe. Alphacore estimates that at least half of the teams will be goners within the first hour. The game will go on for as long as it takes. If you look above your head, each station has a green light just above it, that will turn red when your team is out."

"You better not put those electrodes to your brain today, George. You'll be lobotomized, man." Jamaal said.

"That's exactly what I'm shooting for," George said before lifting his shirt and attaching the electrodes to his nipples.

"OK..." Nick said as he shook his head and popped open a Jolt. "We have 15 minutes to revise our strategy."

"Strategy? It's pretty simple. We gotta be boring, boring as hell," George said.

"He's right. We need to play defense," Jamaal said.

"That's exactly what I was about to say. We let everybody else head-shoot themselves to eternal glory, while we sit back and make s'mores, and then we swoop in to save the day," Nick said, booting up his computer, putting on his headgear and flipping down his visor.

"Hmmm..." I contributed.

"What? You've got a better idea?" Nick asked on the cusp of mansplaining.

"It's just that everybody will be thinking the same thing and employing the same strategy. How can we be different and unexpected?"

"Different will get us killed," Nick said, irritated. "Ready, player one... two, three, and four? Let's hit it." We all spawned into Alphacore and got ready for the mayhem.

Nuffian, Jarno, Girth, and Luna all stood in the town square, with more characters spawning in all the time. Pretty soon, there would be 10,000 of us here, making up the 2500 teams Blondie was talking about—enough to get virtually claustrophobic. Speaking of Blondie, he too had a character, a huge talking-head the size of a small hot-air balloon, hovering above the square spewing instructions and unhelpful anecdotes.

All the teams had access to a rough map of the battle-ground arena—it probably wasn't much bigger than Central

Park, with a central village and scattered farms, industrial complexes, and some forest on the outskirts. It would sure as hell be crowded, at least in the beginning.

"We have another surprise for you!" Blondie's head boomed. The appetite for surprises with this crowd seemed limited, given the subdued reaction. "You are used to being able to use various modes of transportation in Alphacore. I am excited to announce a world premiere! For the first time ever, you will be able to use transportation in the battle zone!" Nerdish gasps from the crowd in Alphacore. "You'll be able to use your trucks, cars, hovercrafts, your tandem bicycles, horses, and mules to kill!" the talking head continued. "You'll find vehicles scattered around the battle arena. Beware, there are not nearly enough for all of you. It's first-come, first-served."

The town square, about the size of four football fields, had been sealed off. We were corralled like cattle. The characters came in all shapes and sizes. There were standard issues characters that looked like they were straight out of a D&D manual, but there were also custom-built characters, some the size of refrigerators with full-body armor, others lithe females with capes, still others, mutants with pig faces and horns and ammo belts strapped across their chests.

All the characters seemed to be coalescing towards the outskirts of the square. No surprise, considering that everybody had three minutes to high tail out of the kill zone. But I wasn't buying it. There must be some other way.

"Let's do the opposite," I said.

"The what?" Nuffian wondered.

"The opposite. Let's go to the middle of the square, while everybody else is going to the edges," I tried.

"That's loco, Luna, we'll be sitting ducks."

"ONE MINUTE BEFORE THE GREATEST BATTLE IN ON-LINE GAMING HISTORY BEGINS!" the head in the sky boomed. "THE WORLD IS WATCHING—MORE THAN 100 MILLION VIEWERS WILL WATCH YOUR HUMILIATION OR YOUR TRIUMPH." A huge counter filled the sky and started to count down towards zero.

We readied our weapons, checked our supplies, and took in the scene—thousands of characters pushed towards the edges of the town square like tweenies at an Ariana Grande concert.

Jarno came to my rescue, "We may be in the top ten percent skill-wise, but given the setup, that doesn't matter much. There are too many factors outside of our control, the stray bullets alone could undo us. It's a mathematical nightmare. I'm with Luna here, we need to be unpredictable."

Nuffian turned towards the head in the sky—30 seconds —and took a deep breath. He lifted his machine gun in one hand towards the sky and turned to us. "Beyond fear!" he shouted, turned, and started to sprint towards the middle of the square. Jarno, Girth, and I turned to each other and smiled. "Beyond fear!" we shouted as we took after Nuffian.

Ten seconds flashed in the sky. We stood back to back, weapons ready, right smack in the middle of the square. Five seconds, three seconds...."GO, GO, GO... TO YOUR DESTINY!" the head in the sky boomed. "THREE MINUTES UNTIL WEAPONS ACTIVATION." Total mayhem erupted as thousands of characters scrambled to get the hell out of town as a new counter appeared in the sky. We stood where we were.

"What now, Luna?" Nuffian asked—not clear if he was being rhetorical.

"We're not going to be alone for long," Girth said, worriedly scanning the horizon.

"Where's the deus ex machina claw from Toy Story when you need it?" Jarno chuckled.

Two minutes to weapons activation. The crowds were thinning out along the perimeter, but there must have been hundreds of warriors milling about, still within the square—a clear and present danger to us. We were utterly exposed. "My thoughts on unpredictability haven't quite germinated yet," I said.

"Great," Nuffian said, almost resigned to his fate.

"So much for being a team leader," Jarno said, checking his

sniper scope. "Oh shit!"

"ONE MINUTE TO WEAPONS ACTIVATION," came from the head in the sky.

"What, what?" Girth said.

"We've got company!"

I heard a wasp-like buzzing in the distance, and then I saw it. A motorcycle with a sidecar was coming straight at us. On board, four seriously messed-up warriors. It looked like a scene straight out of Mad Max, except that these guys couldn't afford a truck. They hung off the speeding motorcycle at various awkward angles, ready to kill.

"Shit, shit, shit, ten seconds..." cried Jarno, throwing himself on the ground and taking up a sniper position.

I raised my MP5. Girth whipped out his weapon. Nuffian nestled his trusted Kalashnikov into his shoulder.

"Good knowing you guys," Girth said.

The motley crew on the speeding motorcycle were closing in fast, with us in their crosshairs. We braced for impact.

"WEAPONS ACTIVATED!"

A roar, a lumbering shadow, a crunch, and the motley crew disappeared in a swirl of dust. We had been so focused on the motorcycle that we hadn't noticed the black semi hurtling in from our left. The team that had hijacked it obviously thought that the motorcycle crew was the bigger threat, and had made a B-line straight for them, wiping out the entire crew in one metal and bone-crushing swoop.

Stunned, we stared at the semi as it began to turn back towards us. I was just about to open up on it when I looked down at my feet. I was basically standing on it, our last best hope of survival in the form of a metal grate. I bent down and tried to pull but it didn't budge.

"Girth! Grenade! Now!" I shouted, pointing to the grate. Jarno was only a couple of feet away from me, trying, and failing, to take out the truck driver with his sniper rifle. Like the pro he was, he didn't question me in the heat of the battle, but simply lobbed a grenade towards me. "Fire in the hole!" I threw myself as far away from the blast as I could. The ground shook. The grate arched high through the sky and came to a clattering stop on the ground a mere foot from me. With our guns blazing, we backed towards the hole and, one by one, dropped down, not knowing what awaited us.

I looked up from the screen. We hadn't been battling for more than ten minutes, but the counter had started to count the dead. We had started at 2500 teams, we were already at 2046. 454 teams wiped out already. I saw red lights dot the hall, indicating which teams had been annihilated. I looked up above me, our light was still green. I knew it would be, but I just wanted to double-check.

Jamaal peeked up too, "I would expect a logarithmic curve. With the death rate steep to start but flattening out, with the last few deaths being the farthest apart."

Back in Alphacore, we were still below ground. The truck maniacs had obviously felt it more important to hold onto their semi than follow us down here. Down here, in the upside-down, it was what you would expect—dank, dark, claustrophobic, and not a little scary.

"Why don't we just take it real slow and let trouble come to us? Every second longer we last, the greater our chances," Girth said as we walked in single-file along a narrow alleyway and into a larger room.

"And the more likely our skills come to play, rather than us being messed up by random shit," Nuffian chimed in from the front. I was bringing up the rear.

Could it really be that easy? Suddenly, Nuffian held up his fist at a right angle to signal us to freeze. "Holy mother," he said. "Frag city here."

The rest of us came up next to him and peered out over the room. There on the ground, in piles, were the dead. There must have been upwards of 20 bodies, freshly fragged. There was something not quite right with the bodies but I couldn't figure it out. Suddenly, a grumbling roar could be heard from the depths of the dungeon.

Girth: "You can't be serious!"

Nuffian: "Bastards!"

Jarno: "No one said anything about NPCs!"

Me: "They're using monsters to flush out hiding wimp fools like us! Not much of a spectator sport if they didn't."

We took a tunnel that led off to the left, away from the roar, and ran. Nuffian first, me second, and Jarno and Girth bringing up the rear. I could sense something behind us, gaining. "Girth, we need some of the grenade action again, please." Girth lobbed a couple of grenades behind us and kept going. The grenades came flying back out of the darkness and detonated not ten feet from us. The blast knocked Jarno and Girth down, and lopped off a sizable chunk of their HPs. I turned around towards them and opened up into the blackness behind them. Sending volley after volley of MP5 rounds at something, I hoped. Nuffian stood beside me and followed suit with his Kalashnikov. Jarno and Girth struggled back up to their feet and staggered towards and passed us.

"We need to get the hell out of this dump," I said as I fired a final round into the blackness and followed them at a run.

CORPORATE BASTARDS

The call came in the afternoon. For once, Tristan was asleep in his bed at home, after working the night shift. He grabbed this cell off the nightstand. "We just got a call from local PD." It was Maria. "A South Asian male was found very much dead in his car, under the 101 overpass. His brains were all over the windshield."

"And you woke me up why?" he asked, realizing as he said it that he sounded like an a-hole.

"According to a preliminary ID, the guy works—worked—for Alphacore."

"Start-up envy? Fomo?" Tristan was already up and pulling on his pants with one hand.

"Suicide ruled out, bullet angle doesn't match. Alphacore's got their own team on it as we speak, backtracking his last few days. This is fresh, blood still warm."

"Remember that head of operations person at Alphacore?" Tristan said, grabbing his shoulder holster. "You know, what's her name..."

"You mean Kalminski?"

The front door of his two-bedroom shut behind him. The hallway was dank and unwelcoming, someone less jaded might even find it threatening, but a federal income and child support payments do not an apartment in Palo Alto afford. He had settled for West Oakland in a two-bedroom. He wanted the extra room should a judge ever allow Charlie to sleep over. His job wasn't exactly nine to five, so his commute wasn't too bad.

"Yeah, right, Kalminski. Call her and let her know we're coming over? I'll start driving now. Meet me in Menlo Park." His car was almost as shitty as his apartment, he noted as he got behind the wheel of his 86 Caprice Coupe. Airbags are for suckers.

"Should we notify Maxwell at intelligence?" Maria asked.

"Now, why would we ever want to do that?"

Local PD homicide had taken the lead on the investigation, which was as it should be. But not much progress could be made without Alphacore corporate. The security guard had reluctantly waved Tristan and Maria through when they had shown their badges at the Menlo Park headquarters. They were led through what looked more like a futuristic playground than an office where actual work was done. There was even more facial hair here than at CGU. They were let into Kalminski's office immediately, not what he was expecting given his previous run-ins with Alphacore Corporate and their lawyers.

Kalminski stepped off the treadmill whirring under her stand-up desk, and met them halfway. She wore black leggings, a hoodie-covered sports bra, and dark hair pulled back in a ponytail. She had a post-workout sheen about her.

"Sorry if we interrupted your workout," Tristan said.

"Casco," she said, "in case you forgot, Alphacore is not an arm of the federal government."

"Last time, you gave us bad intel with crappy consequences for both of us. This time, we need the good intel," Tristan said, getting right to the heart of the matter.

"Our customers count on us to keep their information protected. There is only so much we can give you without breaching that sacred trust."

"Christ, Kalminski, I've heard that one before, and quite frankly, it makes me want to puke. So," Tristan continued, "what was that techie of yours up to? What's his name..." scrolling through his notepad, "yeah, here it is... Ganesh Bail."

"It's only been, what, an hour? What do you expect? We know nothing. We have 5000 programmers."

"Maria!" Tristan shouted suddenly without taking his eyes off Kalminski.

"Right behind you, boss," Maria answered timidly, stepping out from behind him. Renata Kalminski was an icon to some. She'd written some memoir chockfull of unsolicited advice on how women should live their lives and become just like her. As if her lifestyle, with a private nursery attached to her office, and chauffeured cars, could generate insights for a middle-class mother in Bakersfield. Amy had read it just before she left him, he had yet to prove a correlation, let alone a causation, but had his suspicions.

"Maria, tell Kalminski what you told me about Alphacore's future."

"You mean, that thing we picked up?"

"Yeah, that thing," Tristan said.

"What are you getting at, Casco?" Kalminski interrupted.

"I really loved your book," Maria said, "I only have the Kindle edition, or else I'd have asked you to sign it." Kalminski's eyes said 'whatever', so Maria continued. "We've picked up information regarding a possible Microcorp bid on Alphacore," Maria continued.

Kalminski, suddenly not so laid back anymore, said, "What does that have to do with anything?"

Tristan was glad to clarify, "A breach in Alphacore's security, and the possible collateral damage on Alphacore's growth potential among its core demographic? I don't know. You tell me if that has anything to do with anything."

"Are you threatening to leak a confidential homicide investigation?" Kalminski said.

"I don't recall saying anything like that," Tristan said.

Kalminski fell silent for a second, that fast brain of hers doing some quick calculations in order to triangulate the course of action that would have the greatest likelihood of saving her ass. "Listen, Casco," she sighed finally, "all we got so far was that Bail had, before getting his brains blown out, accessed our user data and attempted to identify one, or several, of our players."

"Give me names."

"It's too early to tell."

"We need the information now; those players are exposed and could be in danger. Now, that would be an epic PR disaster, should one of them get knocked off."

"Fine," she sighed, walking towards the door as if to show them out. "I'll get back to you by the end of the day."

"By the end of the day ain't good enough, they'll be dead by then," Tristan said, not budging. His cell buzzed in his pocket. He pulled it out and read the message. He turned to Maria. "I've got to go. Stay here and make sure Alphacore delivers what we need in 30 minutes."

Maria nodded unconvincingly. She was probably not relishing the idea of riding her idol.

GOING ROGUE

ristan checked the message again as he started the Caprice: GO TO OFFICE ASAP R. He drove as fast as the hunk of metal would take him, swerving in and out of traffic and taking a half-dozen illegal turns. The hopeless suspension made it feel like riding butter. Finally, at his workstation, he docked right into the FBI Alphacore office.

Rembrandt was there, waiting for him, among the metal desks and filing cabinets. "What took you so long?" he said. "This place gives me the creeps."

"Sorry to hear that," Tristan answered. "We go above and beyond to ensure a satisfying experience for our taxpayers."

"Just remind me to never set foot here again."

"Spit it out, and you'll be out of here before you know it."

"Remember that AVI file you gave me? Well, we cleaned it up," Rembrandt said while he projected a light onto the nearest wall. "I thought you should see what we found sooner," the cleaned-up film began to play, "rather than later."

Things have a tendency to cluster. Tristan had just logged out of Alphacore when he glanced up and saw Maria come running from the front of the operations room. She was almost out of breath when she reached his desk. She plunked down into her chair and pulled in close to him.

"I didn't want to use electronic communication on this one," she said, recovering from her sprint. "Don't know who to trust nowadays." When he gave her a spit-it-out-look, she got to the point. "We think we've got a name on that dwarf of yours.

The Alphacore forensics team were able to isolate the name that the programmer had leaked before he got his brains blown out." Finally, a break. "The gamer's handle is Luna_tic, and her IP address points us to a street address not more than a couple of hours away, traffic willing."

Tristan was just about to say that they needed to leave now, when he saw Richards come walking down the aisle. He put a hand on Maria's shoulder. "Wait here."

"Her name is Lily," Maria said. "Lily Anderson, she is daughter to—"

"Sam Anderson... Jesus Christ, we should have figured that one out." He turned towards the oncoming traffic. Goddamn it, he's still fidgeting with that thing, it must be a diagnosis, Tristan thought as he met Richards halfway down the aisle.

"Ah, Casco... good job on that sweatshop by the way," Richards said, spinning the fidget spinner. He gestured towards the front of the rooms, "Maybe we should take this in my office."

"I'm on a tight schedule," Tristan said and stood with both feet on the ground, where he was, in the middle of the bustling operations room.

"Things might work out for you here after all," Richard continued. Tristan was in no mood for small-talk. Luckily, Richards got to the signal. "I just got off the phone with the folks at intelligence. They really appreciate the excellent spirit of cooperation we've shown, but their investigation is entering a new phase." Tristan knew where this was going, but he remained stone-faced, so Richards just continued. "They have asked me to ask you to drop it, to back off. I hereby do just that. Back off, Casco."

They say that you are the sum of your decisions. This was never clearer to Tristan than right now. As the trajectory of the rest of his life unfolded before him, he said, simply, "No." He'd be dammed if he were going to fail not just one teenage girl, but two.

"What?" Richards said with genuine surprise, giving his spinner an extra spin. "May I remind you of your station here...

and in life in general."

"Don't you go there, Richards. Christ, I will knock you out cold and stuff that spinner so far up your ass, it will be spinning fecal matter in your mouth," Tristan said matter-of-factly.

"That's it. Thanks for giving me a reason. You're suspended," Richards said, trying not to betray a measure of fear. "Without pay. Hand over your gun and badge."

Without saying another word, Tristan rounded Richards and headed for the elevator. His Glock was snuggly in his shoulder holster and his badge was firmly on his belt. Screw these nerds.

"And the same goes for anyone who helps him!" Richards yelled, his voice hitting unwanted high pitches.

The operations room was quiet as Tristan continued along what suddenly felt like a gangplank, doing his best to control his limp. Tristan reached the elevator and pressed the button. It felt like forever, but finally, the doors slid open and he stepped in. The doors started to slide shut, but then suddenly stopped. A small arm was stuck in between them, and they opened again. There, in front of him, stood Maria with a grin on her face.

Tristan and Maria got out into the parking lot. "You don't have to do this," he said.

"Yes, I do," she replied.

Tristan popped the trunk of his Caprice and pulled out a standard-issue Remington 870 shotgun, and a couple of boxes of rounds. "This is for you," he said, handing Maria the flak jacket. "Where's your car?"

Maria pointed to the faded light-blue Mazda Miata convertible parked a few spaces down. "Christ, this car is older than you. I think you better drive," Tristan said as he squeezed awkwardly into the passenger seat. "Give me your phone." Maria handed hers over. "You still got that address you were talking about?" Maria pointed to her head and nodded. He rolled down the passenger side window and proceeded to throw the phone, together with his own, out of the car's window.

"What are we waiting for?" he said. Maria gunned the engine, as much as the crappy engine really could be gunned, and peeled out of the parking space.

MIATA ON A HIGHWAY

Maria pushed the Miata to the limit across the winding asphalt. Tristan squeezed his left leg and winced. That the car was cramped and damp sure wasn't making things any better. If he hadn't pulled that stunt back at HQ, he would be in an FBI chopper just about now. Maria glanced over at him, "Want to talk about it?" she asked loudly to compete with the road noise.

"About what?"

"About what happened over there."

He sighed, leaned his head back against the headrest, and closed his eyes.

"Bad luck, that's what happened over there."

Maria shifted in her seat uncomfortably, already regretting her question.

"In a previous life, I was part of the bureau's Hostage Rescue Team, believe it or not," he said, motioning to his leg.

"Believable."

"I was embedded with a Delta team in Afghanistan—a knowledge transfer initiative. We were out to catch some terrorists deep in Helmand when everything went to hell."

"I'm sorry."

"You shouldn't be. I knew what I was getting into. Took a bullet to my left thigh here," he said, feeling the scar through his pants. "I was lucky... we lost two that night..."

A year of recovery and rehab followed his return stateside, but the pain in his leg never really went away, neither did the memories of that night—the fear, the confusion, the blood, and the buddies they lost. He was transferred out of the HRT and ended up at the Cyber Gaming Unit. Not exactly a great fit. His marriage fell apart in tandem with his career—the pain killers didn't help.

He opened his eyes again, and to his right, through the car window, he caught a glimpse of the Pacific, the whitecaps stretched all the way across Monterey Bay, Santa Cruz on the other side.

The late autumn sun had just dropped below the horizon when they pulled up to the house. It was in the kind of neighborhood that would forever be out of reach for him. What were the chances that the person they were looking for lived less than two hours from the office? They got out of the Miata, the coke can of a car had done a number on his leg, and for a moment, he thought the leg would let him down completely. Ever since his rehabilitation ended, he had refused to use a cane. He managed to shake off the worst of it. He asked Maria to stay by the car.

He limped up the driveway and rang the doorbell. From the muffled sound, he knew someone was at home. Out of habit, he unclipped his holster and placed his hand on his gun. He took five steps sideways back from the door, just in case anyone inside should be inclined to blast a shotgun through it. After what felt like forever, but was probably just 30 seconds, a striking woman with melancholic eyes opened the door.

He showed her his badge, "Mrs. Anderson?"

"Is it about Lily, again?" she asked.

"Yes."

"One of your colleagues was here not an hour ago."

"Huh, so much for intra-agency coordination," Tristan said as if to laugh it off. "I'm with the cyber gaming unit. Do you have any information about Lily's whereabouts?"

She seemed anxious suddenly. "Like I told your colleague, I don't know where she is. She said that she was going to some event for a couple of days." She hesitated for a second, "I know how it sounds, but—"

"Hey, I've got a teenager too, I know how it is," Tristan lied. He did have a teenager, but he hadn't been allowed to find out how it was to have one.

"Agent Maxwell didn't say anything about her being in danger," she said, suddenly anxious. "Your tone of voice..."

"We don't know if she's in danger," Tristan lied again, "but we would like to locate her as soon as possible. Does she have a cell phone?"

"No, I don't think so, not since Sam died."

Tristan was about to give his cell number to her, should Lily get in touch, but remembered that he had chucked his and Maria's phones out the window. He should've got a burner, but it's too late now, rookie mistake. Telling her to call the FBI field office was not an option.

"Thank you for your time," Tristan said. "I'll let you know as soon as we get any information," telling a final lie. Halfway down the front steps, he turned back, "Wait! Ms. Anderson?" The front door opened again. "Sorry to bother you again, but you don't happen to have a recent picture of her, do you?"

Ms. Anderson left the door ajar as she disappeared for less than a minute. She returned with what looked like a yearbook and flipped it open to a specific page. She tilted the book towards him and pointed, "There she is. This is what she looked like before he died."

"Thank you, ma'am." He took the yearbook from her hands. "I'll get this back to you."

Maria was leaning against the Miata in her baseball cap as he limped down the walkway. He shook his head. She just smiled.

He slammed the car door shut and closed his eyes. "What are you smiling about?" he asked, mostly rhetorically.

"As a matter of fact."

"Well?" he sat up.

"I suggest we head north, to the Moscone."

"The city?"

"Yep, they've got a gathering of gaming nerds there, start-ing today. And it just so happens that our target is one of them." Maria put the Miata in gear and pulled out onto the street.

"How?"

"While you were wasting your time with that milf, I was working the neighbors. Their son is with her. I saw the daughter in the driveway and smooth-talked her. You know, de mujer a mujer."

MASTER CHIEF AND
STAR LORD

"Wait, did I miss something?" Tristan said as he took in the lobby of the Moscone Centre. "I thought Halloween was over already." Gamers were milling about, some in costumes of varying ambition—from your basic cape and helmet, through tight-fitting corsets and thigh-high boots, to full-body suits with integrated electric motors and smoke machines.

"Cosplay," Maria explained. "I used to dabble in it myself, you know, before joining the bureau."

"You seem so competent and rational," he said and smiled. "I keep forgetting you came from this world."

Maxwell could be here already, and considering their rogue status, he wasn't about to announce to the world that they had arrived, so no showing of badge and demanding access. They needed to go stealth. To add a further complication, they weren't registered and didn't have tickets. As he took in the main entrance, he was struck by the excessive perimeter defense—what with a half-dozen refrigerator-sized men in tight black Alphacore t-shirts manning the checkpoint. The men weren't armed as far as he could tell, but they might as well have been.

Tristan tightened the grip on the duffle bag in his left hand. It contained his trusted shotgun. He glanced over at Maria, her eyes lit up as she took in all the characters and the general nerd landscape. Tristan grabbed her by the elbow and led her away from the checkpoint, well aware that he wasn't blending in—he was still wearing his crumpled suit.

He was just turning back around to say something to Maria when he hit something hard and nearly landed on his ass. "Hey! Watch it!" came from behind a military green full-face helmet with a visor. He took in the full-body armor in front of him and grabbed the arm. "FBI, come with me."

"Get off of me, grandpa," armor said and pulled away.

"Nice Master Chief, kid," Maria said. "Is that the prestige model?"

"No way would I buy off the rack," an offended voice came from behind the helmet. "It's 3D printed."

"Of course, I can see that now, the workmanship is sweet," Maria continued, glancing and nodding towards Tristan. "Master Chief, we have a mission for you. A mission of a lifetime."

The stench of the teenage boy was overwhelming inside the helmet, but Tristan didn't have much of a choice. He was now a limping Master Chief—apparently the main character in a game called Halo—in a helmet and full-body (plastic) armor several sizes too small. Maria had somehow managed to smooth-talk the previous owner to part with it. He made a mental note to ask her what it cost her when all this was over. To top that, she'd finagled the kid's girlfriend out of a red Star Lord costume for herself. It came complete with a gray mask and a low, real low, cut top that surely wasn't part of the original. Maria helpfully informed him that Star Lord was a member of the Guardians of the Galaxy franchise, not that it meant anything to him.

"What, you've never seen a pair of these before?" Maria said, pulling at her costume, trying to fit her various body parts in the tightness.

"It's been a while."

"Here," Maria held up two pieces of paper at face level, clearly trying to divert his attention away from her cleavage.

"I've got tickets too."

Tristan stuffed the duffle bag behind a fern standing in a corner of the massive foyer, forlorn and incongruous, a remnant of some past conference—maybe podiatrists. Tristan couldn't swing getting the shotgun past the guards, but his Glock sat nicely in Master Chief's holster. Conveniently enough, Star Lord also has a holster. The guards, distracted by Maria's outfit, just scanned their tickets and let them through without checking identification. They were in.

THE URGE

I don't know how we did it, but somehow, we hightailed out of the upside-down and ended up on a farm in the outskirts of town. It looked like a farm out of a 50s movie, a house, wooden barn, and hay. The difference was the blood. The fields surrounding the farm were strewn with the bodies of the obliterated. Olfactory simulation hadn't yet been incorporated into Alphacore, but I could still smell the blood. We were constantly one step behind the mayhem, a good thing admittedly.

I looked up from my screen with no concept of how much time had passed in real life. The red lights above the computer stations were now in a clear majority, the counter stood at 965 teams left in the game.

"Tell me if I've got this right. Half the teams have been wiped out, and we've barely fired a shot. Where is the honor in that?" I asked.

The smattering of gunfire and thuds of explosions were uncomfortably close. "Be careful what you ask for," Nuffian said as all four of us took cover behind a blown-out harvester. Our map indicated a possible enemy presence in the farmhouse not more than 50 feet from us.

Suddenly, Girth let out a long guttural exhale, sounding almost like a sea lion, as he closed his eyes.

I quickly gripped my MP5 and peeked out from behind the harvester, ready to engage whoever had just hit him.

"Is this really the best time?" Jarno sighed.

I looked over to George IRL on my right. He had his eyes

closed and held one hand between his legs.

"Lazy bastard is pissing in a bottle. It's a bad habit," Nick explained with a smile.

George suddenly jolted back in pain, the bottle almost slipping out of his hand. I could only hope he had finished whatever he was doing.

I quickly turned back to the screen and Alphacore. Girth had been hit—not fatally. "Next time, turn off your volt feedback before taking a leak, you dope," I said.

"Hey, I didn't know they would open fire, and besides, considering the rate at which I've been pounding the jolt, it was bound to happen," Girth said, his voice strained.

I peeked out from behind the harvester and sent a hail of burning metal towards the farmhouse. Nuffian and Jarno also opened fire. Bastards in the house returned fire.

"Just 35 percent of my strength gone. I'm as good as new!" Girth said.

"Girth, you stay here," Nuffian ordered as he chucked two smoke grenades towards the house. "Cover us."

The smoke gave us some cover as Nuffian, Jarno, and I ran for the house. The bullets pierced the smoke around us. "I'll go," Jarno volunteered and whipped out his pump-action shotgun, ideal for close-quarter combat.

"No, I'm going first. I need to kill something, fast," I said as I clapped a bayonet onto my little friend, my MP5.

"Luna!" Nuffian cried and lobbed two grenades through the windows on each side of the front door of the farmhouse, and one at the door itself. Three near-simultaneous bangs and I breached blindly through the door. A wet crunch, and there, mere inches away from my face, was the face of a female warrior with striking elven features. Blood trickled from the corner of her mouth. I looked down to discover that my bayonet was lodged in her chest. I pulled it up into her rib cage for good measure and she let out a final blood-soaked cry. The elven beauty and I stood in the middle of the room, bound together in our dance of death. All around me were sounds of battle.

In the end, the four bodies of the opposing team lay on the floor. Jarno had taken a 50 percent hit. Nuffian and I were unhurt.

"No time for celebration," Nuffian said. "Others are closing in."

I was still in shock over my own bloodthirstiness, it was as though I felt her warm blood on my hands.

"We need to find better cover. What now, Luna? Luna?"

I had stopped listening. For there, in front of me in the supposed real world, in Hall A, not more than 20 feet away from me, he stood. What the hell was he doing here? Had he gotten wind of my own private investigation? Had I been exposed when I visited the FBI Alphacore office?

I toggled off my mic. I nudged Nick. "Don't look up. Just pretend that you're gaming."

"I am gaming! I am actually trying to win," he said.

"Turn your mic off," I instructed him. "The feds are here. Maxwell, the guy who handled my dad's case."

"What! Is he here in Alphacore? That worthless mother. Let me blow him out of the water."

"No, you dope, he is in the next row over, looking right at me, here in SF, California." I kept on pretending I hadn't seen him. "Let's just stay calm and carry on. Don't let him know you've seen him. We need time to think. He probably doesn't want to cause a scene."

"Incoming! Get with it!" Girth cried in my headphones.

"Common ladies! I see two from the west at 180 degrees, behind those trees," Jarno added.

I toggled the mic on again and took a deep breath to regain focus. "Let's roll. No flinching."

LOOK WHO'S HERE

A little while later, with a few more kills to our name, we were in some desolate village. Although night never really came in Alphacore, and the numerous moons contributed a complicated light, some sort of dusk had descended upon us. If there ever had been people in this village, they had fled for a better place a long time ago. They had left in a hurry, leaving the artifacts of their lives behind—a rusted tricycle stood crooked, barely visible in the tall grass that had once been a lawn. In the houses, on the tables set for dinner, the food had rotted and then turned to dust.

I looked up but couldn't see Maxwell anywhere. The red lights in the hall were starting to overwhelm the green lights. I kept my visor on in the hope that it may shield my eyes. As I swiveled around on my chair casually, there was still no sign of him.

"Clear," Nuffian said as he came out of one of the houses.

"For now," I said.

Jarno rested his sniper rifle on a broken fence and used the scope to scan the horizon. Girth looked despondently at nothing much while he fidgeted with his machine gun. The hours of gaming were taking their toll, we were losing focus. Some time to breathe was welcome.

Suddenly, a rustling in some bushes not 20 feet from us. We swung around with our weapons raised and fingers triggered. Girth took out one of his grenades and prepared to lob it into the bushes.

"Wait!" I shouted. "Hold fire!"

"Are you kidding?!" Nuffian countered, "Girth, throw it now, we need to strike preemptively."

"Stop!" I yelled again. Girth looked at me and slowly lowered his arm.

Some more rustling, and out of the bush stepped a cloaked figure.

"Ezio?!" we all exclaimed in unison.

"I don't know who this Ezio person is you're talking about." Ezio continued his approach, an incongruous cigarette still glowing in the corner of his mouth. "But yes, it's me, the guy you met back in good old Rossiya."

I noticed that the others still had their weapons aimed and ready to fire. I guess they were still a bit miffed about last time. "Stand down," I told them. They lowered their weapons, Nuffian most reluctantly.

"Much appreciated. I don't have the powers here that I had over there," Ezio explained. "If you shoot me, I bleed... metaphorically, so to speak."

"What the... how did you?" I tried. I looked up from the screen and out over the hall. "Are you here?"

"The information I have is time-sensitive. I needed to find you. No, I am not in the USA—too many warrants out for me over there."

"What happened to having no interest in helping us?" Nuffian growled.

"But how did you get in? It's a closed server," I said, ignoring Nuffian's petulance and giving Nick a hard slap to the back of the head in real life.

"If there's a will, as they say in America. Really no need to get into details at this point." Ezio took a quick step to the side and an RPG whipped past his head, with only inches to spare, and hit the tree not ten feet behind us. "I think we've got company."

"Incoming from the south at 130 degrees," I yelled. Girth stepped out in front of Ezio, shielding him. Jarno, Nuffian, and I all opened up at the enemy.

I could see at least seven warriors spread out in various covered positions—behind a bush, in the broken window of a house, and crouched in the tall grass. An eclectic assortment of danger. The teams must have entered into some unholy alliance with a temporary common goal—to wipe us out.

"Isn't inter-team cooperation illegal?!" Girth exclaimed.

"Maybe, but what are you gonna do about it?" Jarno said. "Go crying to management?"

"Our overarching objective is to protect Ezio," I found myself saying.

"Uh, winning the tournament on the side would be nice, too," Nuffian said. Could he be jealous?

"We need to back-up into the house, now!" I ordered. Girth and Ezio began to run towards the house nearest to us.

Jarno shouted to me and Nuffian, "You two go, I'll hold them down until you're inside." He took a hit to the leg and got down on one knee, but continued spraying hellfire at the bastards.

We escaped into the fleeting safety of the house. Girth started picking the enemy off one by one with his sniper rifle. Jarno stumbled through the door a few seconds later and joined Nuffian, returning fire through the windows.

I turned to Ezio. "We have no time to lose, this could go either way. Talk."

"We used some methods to improve the quality of the audio and video, and ran some voice and face recognition through it. What we could tell was—" one of the outer walls suddenly collapsed in a cloud of dust and we threw ourselves backward. We retreated into the downstairs bathroom.

Ezio took out a small object from under his cloak, it was the virtual thumb drive he had stolen from me. He flicked a button and pointed it to one of the tiled white walls, then a projection of the video appeared. It was the same video we had seen before, showing the four men in conversation. Only, this time, we could hear and see. "That man there is Gregory Abanov, FSB,

Russian secret service agent and arms dealer with direct ties to Putin." The house shook and tiles fell to the floor around us. "This guy here is CEO of Westcap EnviroTech, Simon Lut." Jesus. My dad's boss. He had been to our house for dinner. "And this is —"

I could hear the rush of blood to my brain. "FBI agent Jonathan Maxwell," I said weakly. I glanced up at the real world. Still no sign of him. Had he been a figment of my imagination?

"Indeed... and based on the furniture, lighting, and partial view out of the window, the meeting likely took place at a Super 8 Motel outside of Campbellsville, Kentucky, in springtime." If Ezio's face could display pride, I am pretty sure it would right about now. "It is pretty obvious that these merchants of death have no idea that they are being filmed. What we don't know is, who was carrying the concealed camera. Only that, whoever it was, wasn't very good at it... an amateur."

"I know who the cameraman is," I almost whispered.

"Luna! We need back-up out here!" I heard cries come from the adjacent room.

I turned back to Ezio, taking a few deep breaths, "We're getting creamed, I don't know how long we can hold them, so if you could cliff note?" As if to emphasize what I just said, the inner wall started to disintegrate as bullets punched through.

"Cliff note?" Ezio asked.

"Never mind, just hurry!"

"They were planning to export weapons technology to Russia, some sort of nano drones," Ezio continued.

"The drones. I've heard about the drones."

"The drones can be used to effectively deliver chemical or biological weapons in a more targeted manner than has been previously possible." A round hit Ezio in the shoulder and he stumbled backwards. "The US has something called the arms export control act. The president, no less, needs to sign off on any deal. Didn't sound like these guys were planning on calling the White House any time..." A second round hit Ezio square in the face and he went down for good.

162

Holy fury overtook me as I understood, finally, the depth of the betrayal... the treason. I could feel my jaw clench in real life as Luna picked the drive off Ezio's corpse and turned to join the ongoing battle. I rushed out into what was left of the living room. I could sense that my teammates were there, barely hanging on, but I didn't stop. I let my rage carry me out into the courtyard. I shot at everything and everyone, pumping lead into anything that moved. I didn't think, I just killed. Had my dad tried to stop this treason, or was he a part of it? I was overcome with shame for even having the thought.

When the dust and blood spray settled, I looked up again from my screen. Maxwell had gone from being a nuisance to being lethal, and I didn't know where he was. Cans of Jolt were littered around me and the pressure on my bladder was becoming unbearable. I wasn't about to do a George and pee in a bottle. Apart from the obvious risks involved when trying to hit a bottle with a vagina, I didn't want to draw unnecessary attention with that whistling sound Sarah had so helpfully pointed out.

I shut off the mic again. "Nick," I nudged his knee with mine. He turned from his screen and looked at me. I did the universal 'cut it' sign, and he cut his mic too.

"Lil, you look like crap," he said. "What did Ezio say?"

"I can't explain now," I said, nausea suddenly supplementing my exploding bladder. Would be a real shame if I short-circuited Speed Freak with my cascading vomit and wet myself at the same time. "All you need to know is that Maxwell is the enemy."

"Oh shit..."

"Yeah, oh shit. He double-crossed my dad and had him murdered," I said, barely believing the words coming out of my own mouth. "Maybe he did it with his own hands."

RAJEEV

I f Tristan was anything, he was a jaded and cynical bastard. What little self-awareness he had was enough to know this. So, he was surprised when his jaw dropped. The landscape of computer screens and nerds stretched out before him was a truly awesome sight to behold. There were thousands of them spread across the floor of the cavernous hall. How the hell were they going to find anyone in this chaos?

Something caught his eye. In a corner of the hall, he spotted the letters FBI on a large rotating rectangular screen hanging over one of the corner booths. "What the hell?" he pointed to the corner.

Maria explained, "It's the new outreach program the PR people cooked up. You know, winning over hearts and minds."

"Christ... good luck with that."

They walked as briskly as possible given their clumsy outfits, over to the corner. They past gamers in intense battles, gamers sleeping heads on keyboards, gamers sleeping on floors, gamers stuffing their faces with Twinkies and Jolt, gamers making friends, gamers flirting. The booth was framed by screens flashing various corny messages about the FBI and career opportunities, with the motto scrolling on one side: Fidelity - Bravery - Integrity. Some glass cases along one wall exhibited tools of the trade, from flak jackets to weapons, to battering rams. A lanky 20-something with a sparse goatee and an FBI t-shirt stood handing out pamphlets to whoever was willing to accept one. One of the passing gamers took a pamphlet, threw it on the ground, trampled on it, and yelled, "You suck, pigs!"

The goatee tried to spin on the impossible, "That's exactly the kind of energy we're looking for! Do you know that the FBI can cover up to half of your student loans?"

Tristan walked up to the goatee and flashed his badge. "We're from the CGU HQ."

"Uhhh... Master Chief," the goatee said, swallowing. "You with the FBI now?" Tristan pulled up his helmet.

"Rajeev," Maria said, reading his name tag. She pulled off her helmet. "Let me be blunt, a girl's life is in imminent danger, and we need all the help we can get. We need to find her, we know she's somewhere in all this."

"Eh... Star Lord? You know I'm a civilian employee, right?"

"So? You've taken the oath, haven't you? You know," Tristan said, raising his right hand. "I will support and defend the Constitution of the United States against all enemies—foreign and domestic."

"Of course, still, I mean, shouldn't you deputize me or something?" Rajeev said, beads of sweat breaking out on his forehead.

Tristan wasn't sure if he was joking or not. "Christ, fine," he said as he approached one of the glass cases and gave it a good smash. As the glass scattered across the carpet, he grabbed one of the FBI badges on display and an expandable baton and a flak jacket.

"You know I had a key for that," Rajeev said, looking at his destroyed exhibit.

"Giving you a gun would probably do more harm than good," Tristan said. "Here is some protection." He helped Rajeev slip on the flak jacket and pinned the badge on to his chest and said, "You are hereby deputized." Then flipped the baton expanding and then retracting it again, and placing it in Rajeev's hand. "A good whack on the head and the perp is out cold, a whack on the arm and the arm breaks, got it? You look like a cosplayer, you'll blend right in."

"Sure," Rajeev said, eyes widening. The poor kid has probably never even skinned his knees, let alone played touch football.

"We are looking for a gamer with the handle Luna, underscore, tic," Maria said. "Real name Lily Anderson."

"Alphacore corporate are not cooperating, citing a lack of warrant and privacy issues." Tristan continued as he unfolded the page he had ripped out of the yearbook and pointed to Lily's picture. "As we have no time for their crap, we need to find her ourselves before the other guys do." Tristan pulled out his Glock 19M, checked that a round was chambered, and re-holstered it, keeping the safety off. He pulled his helmet down. "Let's go."

Seeing the gun, Rajeev hesitated, "I don't get it, why the costumes? Why not just send in the big guns and shut this shit down?"

Tristan stopped, turned back towards Rajeev, and pulled off his helmet again, his hair was already soaked in sweat. He got real close. "I shouldn't be telling you this, but we have reason to believe that the bureau has been compromised." Rajeev's eyes widened. "The fact of the matter is, we have to do this alone, us three." Tristan paused. "There comes a time in every man's life, Rajeev, where a risk has to be taken for the greater good."

Rajeev took a deep breath as if steeling himself. "I understand," he said, serious. He unpinned the FBI badge and slipped it into his pocket. "Probably for the best."

BLOOD SPRAY

Shrapnel whizzed by my head, along with what could have been brain matter. "Luna, goddamnit, haven't we talked about close-range use of explosives?" I looked over at Nuffian, he wiped blood off his face. It wasn't his blood.

"Sorry about that... not." I was still working on rage.

We'd been at it for nearly eight hours by now. It was approaching midnight. JRN had just wiped out yet another team. We had changed our tactics midway through, from defense to all-out offense—which I sometimes took a bit far. Enough teams had been decimated to make it less likely to be knocked out by some stray bullet and for JRN's superior skills to come into play. On the other hand, the teams that were left were, by definition, the best ones or the luckiest ones. I looked up at the sea of red lights, punctuated by the occasional green light. Above me, JRN's green light pulsated mercifully, a beacon of hope. I still hadn't seen Maxwell again. But the hate in the pit of my stomach told me, like a radar, that he was close.

"They could have sort of programmed in a break or two," George said. I glanced over at him. He was looking even less hot than usual, pale and sweaty, shifting uncomfortably in his chair. "I don't know what I would have done without my trusty throne."

The fact that there were no breaks meant that the competition became one of both mental and physical stamina. My eyes were sore, my wrists were experiencing some serious carpal tunnel syndrome, and my neck was so stiff I could barely see my fellow teammates. My brain was on overdrive, but felt like it was running on fumes and could crash and burn any second. I had heard that some of the professional teams had PTs and dietitians on staff nowadays, which suddenly didn't sound that crazy.

Many of the gamers stayed at their battle stations to follow the action, or pick up non-tournament games for consolation prizes. Others milled around the front stage or sat along the stadium seating provided along the sides, catching the action on the big screens. Others were probably off in Hall B scrounging for more loot. Still, others had passed out on the floor or with their heads on the table in front of them. Now that the number of green lights had dwindled, the number on the board stood at 165. Some gamers, eager to get close to the action, gathered around the remaining active battle stations, including ours.

I looked up at the screens on the walls above the main stage. They seemed to show what was being broadcast out to millions of viewers across the globe, selected action from the ongoing battles in Alphacore, cut with shots from real life in Hall A of gamers sweating away at their battle stations, cut with real-life commentators like Monday night football, holding mics and spouting platitudes (I guess as I couldn't hear them). Pictures of the gamers were captured by roaming camera teams and cameras moving along brackets in the sky. The battle scenes themselves were broadcast with a half a minute delay, according to Jamaal, apparently to prevent giving any team an unintentional advantage.

"Yo, guys," I nudged Nick on my left and George to my right. Nick turned and nudged Jamaal on his left. "Strategy session." They all cut their mics and pulled in close. Nick was the nominal team leader, but this was my war, and I was gonna command it.

"So, we are so close to getting out of this round alive," I explained, "and I'm not going to let some treasonous FBI agent ruin it." George glanced over at his screen every few seconds to make sure we weren't waylaid in the middle of our session. "But we need to face the fact that we are fighting a two-front war, in two different worlds."

"Two-front wars have a tendency to end in disaster," Jamaal said. "Just ask Hitler." Nick rolled his eyes.

"As long as this round continues, we are safe," I continued. "I don't think Maxwell wants millions of online witnesses as he carts us off."

"Us!?" George yelped.

"Don't kid yourself, George, we're all deep into this shit," Nick said. "We're a team after all."

I glanced up at one of the massive screens in the front of the hall, and there, suddenly, I saw him. I'm sure of it. He was oblivious to being filmed, but there he was in a huddle with two others. I couldn't figure out where he was from the image on the screen. How am I supposed to fight an enemy I can't see?

George suddenly swiveled away and flipped down his visor. "We're under attack. Engage! Engage!" he cried as his fingers slammed into the keyboard. The other guys did likewise, getting right back into Alphacore. This was crazy.

"Luna, come on! We're getting slammed here!" Nick yelled. I put on my headset and flipped down the visor, just in time to duck as something harpoon-like whooshed passed Luna's head. I looked at my HP, I had less than 50 percent left. Must have been hit without even noticing it.

"Come on! Let's pull back," Nuffian yelled. "See those trees over there, I'll cover."

When JRN were in relative safety again, Nick ripped off his headset and turned to me. "What the hell are we going to do?"

I just shook my head and then stopped. "I think I've got an idea."

There was, by now, a significant crowd around us. Fellow gamers were gathering in the hope of witnessing live one of the top 128 teams finishing. Maxwell must be watching us, but I couldn't see more than six feet in any direction, my view blocked by a wall of nerds. Maybe the nerds can be turned to our advantage.

"You guys, we've got incoming." George looked worriedly at us. "You better get in the game now."

"Yeah, we've got incoming alright. On multiple fronts," Jamaal chimed in.

"Playing for eight hours straight can do a number on your mind," George said. "On one of my 36-hour marathons I started seeing—"

"This is not the time for a story, George," Nick sighed.

I looked up at the giant counter. 147 teams left in the game. Only 19 more teams needed to fall off the face of the earth. "Let's frag these mofos." I lobbed two grenades at the oncoming warriors. "Beyond fear!" I shouted.

"Beyond fear!" the boys replied in unison.

In less than a minute, the ModeratorsXX were toast, so was Girth. Smoke was rising from his contorted body, they'd got him with a flame thrower. George ripped off his headset and reached under his shirt, wincing as he pulled the electrodes off his nipples, and stood up. He was about to walk off when I reached up, grabbed him, and pulled him down hard into his seat.

"No need for violence!" he cried. "I need to take another leak, and you can't expect me to pee in a bottle in front of dozens of strangers, or millions of viewers!"

I toggled off my mic and leaned in close. "Haven't you been listening? Maxwell is here. Whatever the reason, it can't be good. You can't be separated from the group, you'll be too easy a target. We need to stick together." George grimaced, doing everything he could not to grab his crotch. "I'm holding gallons of pee and puke under pressure here too, you don't see me complaining," I said. "Man-up and use your skills."

I glanced up at the counter again. Other teams had been doing their jobs and the number was down to 132. Four teams left to kill. We were fighting fast and loose and taking risks. Jarno was down to 20 percent, Nuffian 35, Luna 48. I looked up at the giant screen and saw myself. Damn, that's the last thing we needed, our mugshots for the world to see. A roaming camera-man was standing not more than ten feet away.

Then, in my headphones, I heard a familiar rumbling. I turned back to Alphacore. Coming right at us, across an open field, was the black semi from the very start of the battle. It was dented, parts were falling off, one tire was out, and it was riddled with bullet holes. But that wasn't about to stop it from running us over. We were nestled behind a couple of boulders, not protection enough against a 40-ton weapon on wheels.

Nuffian was opening up on the remaining wheels of the truck as Jarno tried to sniper the bastard on the roof who was lighting us up with a tripod-mounted autocannon, powerful enough to blast chunks off the boulders.

"Guys, we stay here, we die," I yelled over the sound of approaching death. "Remember the plan!" I shouted. "I'm going." I swung over the boulder in front of me and started to sprint straight for the truck.

The bastard on the roof taking hits from Jarno didn't have time to react and train the autocannon on me. The driver grinned and gunned the truck even harder as he shot through his own windshield, shattering it and hitting me square in the shoulder. I stumbled briefly but recovered, down to 15 percent. The truck was less than 50 feet away now—I didn't have a plan, I just ran on a lethal mixture of adrenaline and fury. The truck was a second from smashing me into annihilation when I slid. I slid feet first, like a baseball player sliding into home plate, under the truck. As I emerged on the other side, I grabbed onto the back bumper. I used the truck's own momentum to swing all the way to the roof of the trailer (lucky that the game's adaptive algorithm even allowed this). I staggered along the roof towards the front. The bastard with the autocannon had no idea what was coming. My combat knife sunk into his throat and his knees buckled as he keeled over and slid off the truck.

Nuffian threw himself out of the way as the truck smashed through the boulders. Jarno wasn't so lucky as the truck slammed him into the ground knocking off the last of his

HPs. "Shit!"

I clung on for dear life while the truck swung back to finish Nuffian off. I regained my footing and grabbed the autocannon mounted on the roof of the trailer with both hands. I aimed it downwards and into the truck's cabin below and let her rip. The sound was overwhelming as 20 MM explosive round after 20 MM explosive round punched holes into the cabin's roof. The truck started swaying uncontrollably as blood spray blew out of the holes in the cabin like water out of a whale. I jumped off, landing hard and knocking off nearly all my HPs, just before the truck smashed into a grove of trees,

The crowd gathered around us went wild. I felt hands slapping me on my back. I pulled my eyes out of Alphacore and onto the giant screen in front of me. I saw Luna firing into the cabin on the 30-second delayed loop and heard the even larger crowd upfront in Hall A roar. The counter stood at 128. JRN had survived to fight in the next round—now all we had to do was survive in real life.

I flipped up my visor, ripped off my headset, and turned to Nick. His eyes met mine, sweat trickling down from his hair onto his temples. He nodded. Jamaal, to Nick's right, was already in motion. He was on his feet and moving in to shield me and Nick. George was a bit slower, but did the same on his side. They had their backs to us looking for the enemy. We had no plan for what to do if they encountered said enemy. The crowd was still closing in on us, some of the nerds even going in for hugs. Blondie yelled something into the sound system, but I couldn't take in what he was saying. I cast around wildly trying to find Maxwell, or one of his henchmen, but all I saw were pasty white kids with various stages of failed facial hair. I grabbed Nick's hand. We counted to three and then we were gone.

We slid off our chairs, down into the cable jungle below, and began a long crawl under the row of tables that stretched to the aisle. We dodged cables, shoes, soda cans, half-eaten protein bars, legs, sleeping gamers, and wet patches that were better not to linger on too long. Behind us, something crazy was going down, but we couldn't stop to figure out what it was.

I crawled ahead and Nick brought up the rear. Speaking of rears, for a second, while fleeing for my life, I worried about how my rear might look to Nick as he crept behind me. I should have upgraded my jeans before going to the tournament. The row was coming to an end. I saw legs pass along the aisle. This was about as far as our plan had taken us. Which way to run?

MOSH PIT

Tristan heard the crowd go wild in the hall. He had no idea why, but there were a hell of a lot of excited nerds milling around. How were they supposed to find Luna-_tic in this mess? Tristan as Master Chief, Maria as Star Lord, and Rajeev as Rajeev, had decided to split up. They started asking around if anyone knew where Lily or Luna was. They'd been at it for at least 20 minutes when, as Tristan turned into one of the countless rows of kids in front of computers, he was knocked sideways. His Master Chief helmet slid up and off his face. "Hey! Watch it, Bozo," someone yelled as Tristan grabbed the helmet just in time and pulled it back down over his face. He looked up and saw a face full of disdain and hate and, maybe, fear—Maxwell.

Maxwell continued right past him, clearly in a hurry and with a goal in mind. A couple of thugs, with crew cuts and bulging muscles under t-shirts and lousy leisure suits, were right behind him. They gave Tristan a shove just for good measure as they passed. Tristan briefly saw himself pull out his Glock and fire a hail of slugs into all three backs—an unproductive yet satisfying fantasy.

Tristan swiveled around in his plastic suit of armor just in time to see Maxwell charge into a sea of nerds like a bowling ball into pins. Nerds started to fly outward in arches to the left and right. But as one nerd was removed, two nerds came running to replace them. Total mayhem ensued, compounded by Alpha-core corporate security in tight black t-shirts, like some fascist paramilitary group, joining the fray on Maxwell's side.

It was risky, but Tristan had no choice... he had to go in, for Lily's sake. The helmet made it hard to see, let alone fight, but he could still tell the difference between good and evil. He was discreet about it, slamming his fist into fascist kidneys, felling one security guard after the other as he made his way to where he thought Maxwell might be. By the time he'd reached the center, what security guards were left standing had formed a perimeter, behind which he saw Maxwell choke-holding a pasty fat gamer, and one of his leisure suite thugs was pushing some scrawny gamer's face into a table while twisting his arm behind his back. The screams of enraged nerds trying to breach the perimeter made it impossible to hear what was being said. One of the nerds just in front of him took a swing at a guard with a keyboard and was immediately felled by a Taser to the neck. It became clear that these nerds had some pretty serious pent-up anger issues when a computer monitor came flying from behind Tristan, hitting a guard in the head and knocking him out cold. This only served to egg other nerds on, and more objects came flying, from cans to mice, to chairs.

Tristan could see that none of the gamers Maxwell had in his hands were Lily, let alone female. One of the thugs tapped Maxwell on the shoulder and pointed to the giant screen at the front of the hall. There, on the screen, was the girl in the yearbook picture. She ran past a camera, followed closely by some other kid. She was older, thinner, and sadder, but it was her. Maxwell let the pasty kid go and proceeded to extricate himself from the crowd, taking down any nerd that got in his way. He butted heads, elbowed faces, and kicked gonads on his way out, passing not five feet from Tristan.

Tristan was just about to follow when he felt a crack to the back of the head and went down. On the floor, he had a second to think that it must have been one of the guards he had punched in the kidney that got him when he was slammed in the stomach and nearly passed out. He looked up from the floor, all around him, a mosh pit of nerds and guards. One particularly angry guard stared right down at him with a foot in the air ready to stomp him in the face. Tristan squeezed his eyes shut and braced for impact, all the while cursing himself for his carelessness, for taking his eyes off the ball, for his general ineptitude, for not fighting hard enough for Charlie, and for not being the one who died in Helmand. But the stomp never came.

Instead, Tristan was pulled off the ground by both arms. "Let's get the hell out of here," Maria smirked. He nearly tripped over the bloody face of the guard as Maria led him swiftly through the crowd. He looked back, a shell-shocked Rajeev was bringing up the rear. Tristan could barely keep up, something was wrong with his leg, something worse than usual.

BEYOND FEAR

Those damn cameras wouldn't let up. We crouched along row upon row of battle stations. My brain was still tingling with the mental watermark of victory—like I had just walked out of an Avengers movie with the conviction of infinite possibilities. I hadn't felt like this since on the water with my dad. It would be a shame to die now.

I thought of George and Jamaal doing exactly as they said they would do, going beyond fear for the team. Going beyond fear for me, and meeting the enemy head-on, with honor. We still had no idea where we were going. I don't believe in fate, but I felt like something was guiding me, like someone was protecting me.

We came to where Hall A and Hall B intersected. I swung left instinctively, and pushed through two tall black doors marked 'Do Not Enter'. We stopped cold as the doors swung closed behind us. Silhouettes of masts stretched out before us like a forest in nuclear winter. Hulking sailboat hulls towered in rows, their centerboards hoisting them into the air precariously like a giant's domino run. The boat exhibit lay deserted and dark. The only thing breaking the silence was a slight clucking as if there was a body of water somewhere in here.

"Come on," I whispered and pulled Nick along the carpeted aisles. I was thinking tactically like I didn't know I could. I must have honed the skill in Alphacore without ever realizing that it could come in handy in real life, like when you're being hunted by a homicidal federal employee. I kept thinking, escape route, vantage point, weapon, high ground, element of surprise, overwhelming deadly force.

I must have been to the boat show at least a half-dozen times. The club got free tickets, and my dad and I used to go and dream. We dreamt of sailing around the world, just the two of us, and would walk down the different aisles making fictional purchases of all the sailing stuff we would need: life raft, man overboard module, water maker, submersible emergency pump, sonar, radar, satellite phone, ham radio, autopilot, binoculars, fishing gear. And, of course, a boat. A 50-foot beauty that could carry us through the roaring 40s and furious 50s of the Southern Ocean, help us outrun pirates in the Indian Ocean, and dodge supertankers in the Singapore Strait. We would snorkel with amberjacks and yellow-tailed grunts off the Galapagos, run on the endless beaches of the Maldives, round Cape Horn on Tierra del Fuego, and anchor off Sydney Opera for lunch. All dreams of a life with my dad... a life that was no longer mine. A life that had been stolen from me.

We had just turned down the water sports aisle, somewhere in the middle of the exhibit, when I heard Maxwell behind us.

"Lily! Come on now. I know it's you."

I wasn't about to waste my home court advantage. We stopped in front of the fishing gear. In one of the cases lay a beautiful mahogany spear gun. No one had bothered to lock the case, so I just slid the door open and grabbed the gun. It had a two-foot steel-tipped spear set sweetly in its rail. I pressed the butt of the gun against my stomach and, with about as much force as I could muster, pulled back the two heavy-duty rubber slings. The gun was ready to fire.

"Here, this one's for you," I handed Nick the spear gun.

"Gee, thanks!" he whispered. "What do you expect me to do with this?"

"Use it." I handed Nick a spare spear. "In case you miss."

"Miss what?"

I heard Maxwell again, closer this time. "Just hand over

the key, Lily! That's all we want! We won't hurt you!"

We rushed past fishing poles, tackle, fins, wet suits, tubes, wakeboards, surfboards, and water skis. Finally, we came to what I'd been looking for—the safety aisle. We were halfway down the aisle when I stopped. I pulled on one of the cases, this one was locked. That wasn't going to stop me. I kicked the case, the lock broke off with a pop loud enough to give away our location. I grabbed the biggest flare gun I could find and stuffed a handful of flares in my pockets. I wasn't sure if you could actually kill anyone with a flare gun. I think I might have heard of someone shooting a charging bear with one once. But would it stop a charging, corrupted, lethal, bastard of an FBI agent?

"Let's go," I said as we set off again, weaving down the aisles. I heard steps and voices behind us, sometimes close, sometimes far away.

"Is that him?" Rajeev asked, pointing to the giant screen above the main stage. They saw a man in a suit, filmed from above and behind, push through two giant black doors followed by the two goons.

"Damn if it isn't," Tristan said, surprised at his own luck. The picture cut away to show some random kids. They scanned around them, desperately trying to match what they had just seen on the screen with their own surroundings.

Rajeev pointed toward the back of the main stage, "Looks like it's this way." They rounded the main stage and kept going toward Hall B, weaving in and out of nerds as they went. Just before they reached Hall B, they stopped, and there in front of them were what looked like the doors they had seen on the screen.

As the three of them stood at the doors, ready to push in, Tristan realized to his dismay that Maria wasn't wearing her flak jacket. She hadn't got it to go with her Star Lord outfit. Maxwell had murdered twice, at least, and wouldn't hesitate to do it again. He looked at Rajeev, pathetic with his baton.

Tristan pulled off his helmet, his hair wet with sweat. "I

don't know who the two tag-alongs are, but they dress, walk, and smell like Russian special ops."

Maria ripped off her own mask, her cheeks were flushed and her skin glistened. She unholstered her Glock. "What are we waiting for?" she said, glancing at the tall black doors.

Tristan unholstered his own weapon and shook his head, "I'm going in alone, it's just too dangerous."

Maria gave him an incredulous and defiant look, flipped off the safety, and chambered a round. "Like hell you are," she said.

"I have nothing to lose, you have everything to lose," he said.

"What about your daughter, doesn't she deserve a dad?"

"Maybe, just not this one."

Maria let her eyes move across his face, "Self-pity doesn't become you," she said matter-of-factly, and then, without saying another word, pushed through the doors and disappeared.

"Shit!" Tristan said as he turned to Rajeev. "You need to stay here. You have fulfilled your oath."

"But—" Rajeev tried.

"You now need to bear witness." Tristan ripped off the top of his Master Chief suit, he didn't need to hide anymore, and bent down to his right ankle holster. He took out the drive where he had put the video Rembrandt had cleaned up. "If we don't get out of here," he placed the drive in Rajeev's hand, "you need to give this to Miroslav Latki, with SFPD. Do not let anyone else know you even have it." Rajeev nodded and Tristan turned and pushed through the doors into relative darkness. It took him a few seconds to realize what he was looking at—a sea of boats without the water.

"Lil," Nick whispered, "I know you're pissed and all, but shouldn't we call the cops or something?" We had left the safety aisle behind us and were crouched behind the Sunseeker meeting room, where high rollers meet to discuss multimillion-dollar yacht deals over glasses of champagne. The massive fiberglass dreams rising more than 20 feet high, all around us.

"He is the cops," I hissed. "Besides, we don't know who we can trust. We have to deal with this now. I just don't want to run anymore..."

"But he's a maniac."

"Maybe, but what he doesn't know is that I'm a lunatic."

"Great, I'm stuck between a maniac and a lunatic," Nick sighed, only half-jokingly. We were both soaked in sweat.

My anger had worked wonders in Alphacore, pushing JRN to new heights, carrying us all the way to the finals. My anger had now reached a new level of intensity, but would it be a match for real bullets?

Maxwell was becoming increasingly careless. "Hey, kiddo, I just want to talk, I promise nothing is going to happen to you." By babbling incessantly, he was divulging his own position. It was impossible to tell for sure, but it sounded like he was less than 100 feet away now. "Your mother is worried. I spoke to her earlier. I'm sure we can work all this out." So, he was threatening my mom now. On the positive side, he wasn't scared of me—a tactical mistake for him but a tactical advantage for me. I gripped my flare gun tight, still not entirely confident in its effectiveness as a combat weapon. Since when is a Reddit thread on shooting bears with flare guns something to bet your life on? If I could find a way to leverage it. "Your father wouldn't have approved." That's it. The bastard just sealed his own fate.

"What about the other guys?" Nick whispered.

"What other guys?"

"Didn't he have like two henchmen with him?"

I had been so focused on Maxwell that I completely forgot to factor in his posse. Rookie mistake. They could be flanking us right now. Nick was gripping the spear gun. He had killed thousands in Alphacore, headshot records and all, but could I count on him to kill for real? Could I count on myself to kill for real?

I rested the back of my head against the cool glass of the Sunseeker booth and looked up at the beamed ceiling some 40 feet above us. The random shadows and blue-tinged light that danced across it harmonized with the faint but familiar cluck-ing sound in the distance. I looked down at my flare gun again, "I know what we need to do," I whispered to Nick.

Maria was crouched low just to the left of the door. The exhibit hall was massive, and a tactical nightmare. There were hun-dreds, if not thousands of places to hide. The advantage lay with those who stayed put, but Tristan and Maria needed to keep moving. He thought he heard a voice somewhere at the other end of the exhibit hall. He crouched down next to Maria. "They are at least three," he whispered. "We have to assume that they are armed and prepared to use deadly force."

"Shoot to kill, got it," Maria said, reading his mind.

"We're gonna have to split up to cover this place. You take the left flank and I'll take the right." Maria nodded. The main lighting in the exhibit hall was switched off, but many of the booths and boats had their own lighting on. Darkness punc-tured by points of light.

Maria was just about to set off when he took hold of her arm. He could feel the warmth of her sweat between his fingers. "You don't have to do this," both hoping and not hoping that she would change her mind.

"Asshole," she scoffed and shrugged him off, "we've al-ready been over this," and was on her way.

"This isn't a Bond movie, I'm not going to drive a hovercraft right at the enemy," Nick whispered through clenched teeth. We had scrambled our way past the massive luxury gas-guzzling motorboats towards the far corner of the exhibition hall and the clucking and the blue light. The carpeted exhibits helped us move stealthily, but I couldn't shake the feeling that we were surrounded. Then we heard him again.

"I don't want to have to call in the cavalry, Lily," Maxwell's voice was closer now. "I can't control the cavalry, or the level of violence they will direct at you, and that friend of yours, or should I say boyfriend."

"He's bluffing," I whispered to Nick. I knew he wasn't going to call anybody. He was a treasonous bastard who needed to watch his own back, all the while trying to stick a knife into ours. His desperation was our advantage.

I had finally found what I was looking for. Our backs were against cool glass again, but this glass was even cooler because, behind it, were thousands of gallons of water. The glass walls rose six feet to enclose an artificial indoor lake on which to demonstrate hovercraft and jet skis. All this water was too much to bear. My bladder was about to explode. I had started to slow-drip into my underwear. "Turn away," I ordered Nick.

"What?"

"Turn around and don't dare turn back before I tell you to." I gave him a look that made it abundantly clear that I was deadly serious.

"I don't get it, but ok," he said wearily and turned away.

I slid over a few feet along the wall.

"And cover your ears."

"What?"

"Cover your ears or I will shoot you in the face with our flare gun."

He sighed and did as he was told.

I pulled down my pants and underwear, crouched, and, finally, released. It was bliss. The bliss was muddled by that damn whistling sound. It was louder than ever, and, for a second, I thought of how pathetic it would be if I was found dead on the floor, pants down, betrayed by my own bodily functions. I pulled up my pants, scooted back over to Nick, and gave him a tap on the shoulder. I saw in him that he knew what I had just done.

"If they drive hovercrafts here, what do they need?" I asked in a whisper.

"I don't know, a driver?"

"Gas, you dope... and why do we like gas?"

"Uhh..."

"Because we can set it on fire. We just need to find it."

We ducked along the edge over to the back of the water tank, in the far corner of the boat exhibit. An emergency exit's green light beckoned us, offered us a way out. But did it really? Maybe my judgement, my risk assessment, had been impaired by the hours of gaming, playing games where the risk-reward ratio was skewed. Whatever the reason, I was convinced that I needed to take a stand, here and now, that I needed to stop running, and I had just spotted what I would need to do it. There, against a wall, stood a heavy-duty fire locker... the type to store lawnmower gas at a Home Depot. I felt the locker door, praying that it wasn't locked. It opened up to reveal its valuable contents, a dozen or so gas cans in red plastic.

We pulled out one five-gallon gas can after the other and carried them to the front of the water tank. We worked in stealth mode, unsure how close Maxwell was as we placed the fuel tanks, evenly spaced in a semicircle of about 20 feet in radius around us.

I had just put down the last can when a crash came from somewhere in the middle of the exhibit. We took cover behind a couple of jet skis displayed close to the water tank. I thought of Jamaal and George, may they be safe.

"I know you're here." Maxwell's voice was really close now.

Maxwell's voice echoed in the distance. Tristan used the voice as a homing device. His leg was aching, he couldn't remember when he had gone this long without sitting since Helmand. The crouching was killing him to the point that he had to stand up straight most of the time, making himself an easy target. He was surrounded by dozens of out-borders on various mounts—Yamaha, Mercury, Honda, Evinrude, Nissan...

Then, suddenly, he heard a muffled cry far to his left, a thud, a crack, and then another thud. He ran towards the sound as fast as his body would take him. His leg was almost scraping behind him. He figured that the sound was coming from a point where Maria would be just about now if they had kept pace.

He zigzagged between the out-borders and past a wide carpeted walkway that, he guessed, ran down the middle of the entire exhibit hall. He ran past the tackle booths and rows of fishing rods. He heard a crash just feet away.

He rounded a cluster of windsurfing sails, and there he saw them. To his right, no more than 30 feet away, one of the henchmen had his hands around Maria's neck. He had pushed her up and into an upright glass display case, her feet were off the ground, kicking wildly, as she was fighting for her life. Tristan raised his Glock and aimed right at the henchman's head.

"Let her go," Tristan said calmly but clearly. This was an easy shot, even if he only had one useful leg to stand on. His finger started to squeeze the trigger. He would have preferred to handle the situation without firing a shot as the noise would bring unwanted attention from several directions, but he couldn't wait any longer. "Last chance, let her go."

"Drop it," came a voice with a Slavic lilt. Tristan glanced to his left, and there stood henchman number two. Maria's legs were still kicking, but she would pass out any second now. The henchmen had obviously also been given instructions regarding noise levels, or else he would be dead already. "Drop it, now." Tristan released the pressure on the trigger and was about to disengage the target, but something he saw made him hesitate. It was a gamble, but they were both dead if he didn't try.

"How's about *you* drop it," Tristan retorted.

Henchman two's eyes widened, he hadn't expected this. He looked like he was about to abandon his instructions and fire anyway. Tristan returned attention to his target, the bastard who was choking Maria. He squeezed the trigger to the brink and waited, and waited... until he heard a crack to his left and fired. The henchman's head exploded as he went down like a sack of potatoes, bringing Maria down on top of him.

Tristan looked to his left. Henchman two lay in a tangled pile of limbs. Rajeev stood over him with a bewildered look on his face, and that beautiful baton in his hand.

IGNITION

"**I** know you're here, Lily," Maxwell's voice sounded like he was right next to us. "Or should I call you Luna... isn't that what your dad used to call you?"

I looked at Nick, he looked at me. That somewhat lost look he had been carrying for the last half-hour had dissipated and been replaced by determination.

A familiar frame stepped out of the shadows. He'd found us. "Great to see you again, Lily," he said, that eternal gum still in his mouth. "What's it been, a couple of months?"

Nick lifted the spear gun. He looked over at me, I nodded slightly.

"Not nearly enough," I said as Nick aimed and fired. The spear shot out of the gun, hit, and glanced off the gas can that stood two feet to Maxwell's left. Maxwell, unfazed, even amused, took a step forward. "Your father was in way over his head. He didn't understand how things work in this world. He was naive, that's what he was. His fate was an inevitable extension of this fact. You see... the forces that guide our world will not be deviated. They are inexorable."

I gripped the flare gun behind my back as Nick struggled next to me to load the spear gun. I couldn't blame Maxwell for believing that he was witnessing amateur hour. Nick managed, finally, to pull back the heavy-duty rubber bands and place our last spear in the rail.

"One could argue," he continued, "that we should have known... that I should have known that it was you all along. But you seemed so weak, so pathetic in your wallowing. I was convinced that you were a coward like your father." Suddenly, another crash, this one closer. Sounds of things breaking, a struggle, somewhere in the shadows. Maxwell didn't flinch. His focus was all on me. Nick raised the spear gun again. Maxwell just grinned. Nick pulled the trigger and the spear was catapulted along the rail and off the gun, right into the gas can. Maxwell didn't even bother to look as gas started to stream out of the hole, puddling around it and spreading outwards until Maxwell was standing right in it. He thought Nick had missed.

I have always loved the smell of gas. My dad and I had a ritual on those sailing Saturdays. On our way to the club, we would stop at the local 76 on Lucas Ave. My dad let me fill her up. When I was a kid, he used to stand right behind me, his hand on mine, to make sure that the muzzle didn't slip out. Later, he would simply lean against the side of the hood, strong arms crossed in front of him, a smile on his face like he could stand there forever, just looking at me as I focused intently on not messing up. We always paid inside the shop so that we could pick up one slush puppie each. Mine was red. His was blue. They tasted the same—like crap. But we didn't care.

I had seen the movies. I knew I was supposed to say something cool, or profound, or humorous. I skipped all that and I simply raised my flare gun. Maxwell saw it for what it was, a harmless tool for shipwrecked sailors.

"For the last time, Lily," Maxwell said, finally pulling his own gun from its holster, "give me the key. I have shown restraint, but my patience is running out in tandem with your chance of getting out of here alive."

"Beyond fear," I said calmly and fired. The flair shot out of the plastic barrel and hit the ground right in front of Maxwell, and... nothing. It just lay there, spreading its bright red light, making Maxwell look like the devil he was.

I glanced over at Nick, his mouth was open. I looked back at Maxwell, his gun was raised and pointed at Nick. "Give it to me now." I looked down for a second to fish out the drive from my condom pocket when, suddenly, a shot rang out. I froze, my eyes on the floor. I dared not look up. He had brought me back from the brink, he had invited me into his home, he had a kind smile, he'd built me Speed Freak, and opened up a new world. Now he was dead, and it was all my fault.

"Check him," Tristan ordered Rajeev and pointed to henchman two as he ran over to Maria and pulled her off henchman one and lay her on the ground. She was badly hurt, bruised around the neck, and blood in her hair, but she would survive. She had the energy enough to give him a smile. He smiled back and stroked hair from her forehead.

"He's dead," Rajeev said, now standing next to him. "I killed him."

Tristan was about to say something moderately consoling to him when a rattle of gunshots rang out from the corner of the hall, not far away, followed by a loud crash.

"Rajeev, you stay here with Maria," Tristan commanded. "We have no choice but to call for help now. Start with the SFPD and the EMS. Request multiple ambulances." Rajeev just nodded, his hand on Maria's side, looking over at the body of the hench-man whose head he'd just split open. "You did good," Tristan assured him. "You did what you had to do." Tristan turned and started towards the direction of the gunshots. He was met by a wave of ankle-high water. He figured that the water's source was where he was heading. His leg was now officially useless, drag-ging behind him in the water. If he could saw it off to go faster, he would.

When I finally dared look up, I saw Nick still standing there, very much alive—for now. The rush of relief nearly made me forget where I was until my eyes fell back on that familiar smirk now spread across Maxwell's face. "Hand it over," he said with an icy calm, motioning with his left hand while his right still held that gun. We were out of options. I wasn't about to let Nick die for this... for anything. I held out the drive in the palm of my hand for Maxwell to take. He took a step towards me, and then, he lit up.

He lit up, figuratively, at the thought of getting what he wanted, and then a second later, literally. The flare finally did what it was supposed to do, ignite the gas that had pooled around Maxwell's feet. Nick and I just stood there, frozen. It was an awful and wonderful sight. Maxwell, the human torch, flailed as the flames leaped up his cheap suit, and his face and hair caught fire.

Then, his gun went off. Nick and I hit the ground as bullet after bullet smacked into the thick glass behind us. Cracks spread throughout it like a spider's web until, finally, the glass couldn't take it anymore. The glass gave way with a crack and a wall of water exploded out towards us. The roaring water knocked over everything in its path, including me. As I went under, something big swooshed past me mere inches above my head. I lost sight of Nick and Maxwell in the swirl of water and debris. It felt like I was stuck in a washing machine, or at least what I imagine it might feel like. Finally, I broke through the surface and gasped for air. I came crashing to a stop against a canoe that was wedged between two booths. I stood up, soaked, knee-high water still swirling around me. I felt the familiar taste of iron in my mouth and touched my hand to my head; my hand came back red. All around me was mayhem, alarms were blaring, lights were flashing. Where was Nick?

Just when I needed all the oxygen I could get, I held my breath. A figure emerged from behind one of the booths, limping through the debris-ridden water. I felt instinctively for a weapon that I didn't have, and opted for the next best option. I turned to run.

"Lily! Wait!" the figure shouted and whispered at the same time.

I didn't, wait.

"Remember the clowns?" he continued.

I stopped and turned back around. "Skulder?"

"Who?"

"CGU?"

He nodded.

"It's about freaking time," I said.

"Where's Maxwell?"

"Last time I saw him, he was on fire," I said. "I lost Nick."

She was bleeding from the head, but it didn't seem to bother her, so Tristan didn't let it bother him either. He was on the hunt for Maxwell with a lethal weapon in his hands. Having a deranged teenage girl tagging along was suboptimal, to say the least, and not in keeping with agency policy.

He made a half-hearted attempt at talking some sense into her. "Stay here until the cops get here."

"I've got to get to Nick," she said. "I put him in this situation, it's up to me to get him out of it."

Any minute now, the place would be swarming with cops, he wasn't entirely sure if that was a good thing. His gut told them that he needed to find Maxwell before anybody else did. He felt for his left ankle, and, against his better judgement, relieved his ankle sheath of its three-inch knife. "If you insist, you might as well take this." He had already handed a weapon to one civilian today, with good results. Why not double down on that bet? Besides, he wasn't about to let her go into a battle unarmed. He handed the blade to Lily. She took it, felt its weight and its balance in her hand for a second, gripped it, and, without saying a word, began to walk, steps squelching, back towards the water's source. The water had, by now, receded, leaving a field of sodden trash and waterlogged carpet behind it.

Tristan did his best to keep up. He might as well let her lead the way—he didn't have any better ideas. They hadn't gotten much further than 30 feet when, suddenly, a rasping sound came from their left, pushing through the wailing sirens. Lily set off on a run straight for the source. Tristan tried to follow.

I smelled the burnt flesh before I saw it. As I rounded what was left of a demolished booth, I saw them. Maxwell must have heard me and swiveled around to face me. He held Nick pressed close with an arm around his neck. He bored his pistol into Nick's temple. Nick looked like one could expect... like he was having a really, really bad day.

A horrifying gasp was all that came out of Maxwell's mouth, or what was left of it. His face had melted partway off his skull, and what was once a mouth was now just a gaping hole from hell. His beady eyes were still more or less intact. He didn't have to say anything. I knew what he wanted, and I didn't have it. The drive was gone, lost in the tidal wave. But I wasn't stupid enough to let him in on that little secret.

I could sense Skulder limping up behind me. He pulled up next to me and I could see from the corner of my eye that he raised his gun and aimed it at Maxwell. "Let him go," Skulder said calmly.

In an implausibly elegant move, Maxwell swung Nick around in half a turn so that Nick's back was towards us and I could hardly see Maxwell at all. The gun was in Nick's mouth. I couldn't see it, but the sound of metal against teeth and Nick's throttled gasp. There was no way Skulder could get a clear shot now.

The thumping of rotor blades was as clear an indication as any that they had entered the endgame. Maxwell wasn't about to leave any witnesses behind. If he didn't get what he wanted within the next few seconds, the poor kid with the gun in his mouth would be toast. Getting in a 20-foot shot like this one would normally be a cinch. He'd have to hit Maxwell more or less right between the eyes to knock out his central nervous system, to make him drop instantly and prevent him from voluntarily or involuntarily pulling the trigger. But Tristan could barely see Maxwell at all. The coward was hiding behind a kid. Another, admittedly risky, option would be to shoot the kid, somewhere soft and nonlethal, and hope for the best. Hope that the slug would continue through him and come out the other side, and in turn, hit Maxwell. A geometrical crapshoot he wasn't prepared to gamble on.

"Let the kid go," Tristan tried again. "I'm sure this can be worked out. Just let him go."

Tristan glanced over at Lily no more than two feet away from him. It was like she was on automatic, intently focused on the scene in front of her. He could see that she was holding the knife he'd given her in her right hand, but it wouldn't be much use to her now.

"Luna," a garbled wheeze of scorched lungs came from the hole in Maxwell's face. "Your dad begged... for his life. He cried like... like a baby."

I could feel my hand squeeze the knife's handle, letting the steel fuse with my body and become one. For a moment, rational doubt fought back, reminding me that this wasn't Alphacore. Reminding me that we were, instead, in a world where actions have real consequences... a world where you die when you run out of HPs... a world where daughters have fathers ripped away from them. But rational doubt lost. I charged. I ran toward Maxwell and Nick with the knife in my hand, with no plan for what to do when I got there.

In an instant, the playing field changed. Lily sprung forward like a pouncing mountain lion. Tristan had to factor yet another parameter into an already complicated situation. His Glock was raised, his finger on the trigger, ready to blast Maxwell's head off. Lily had covered half the distance between her and Maxwell in less than two seconds. Nick fell away from Maxwell and Tristan squeezed the trigger to the brink and flinched. In his sight was the wrong head—Lily's head.

The waterlogged carpet squelched under my feet. I could glimpse Maxwell's brow-less eye widen from behind Nick as he saw me coming for him. He hesitated, there was less than ten feet between us now. I was still gaining speed when Maxwell heaved Nick out of the way to liberate his gun from Nick's mouth. I caught a glimpse of the muzzle in his hand, and then, suddenly, I went down. A second later, a shot rang out.

Tristan set off after Lily, he couldn't let her go into hand to hand combat alone. He ran with his gun still aimed at where he hoped Maxwell's head would appear. This meant, effectively, and not a little worryingly, that he was still aiming at the back of Lily's head. A split-second later, Lily disappeared, and in her place, right in his line of fire, was Maxwell's melted face. Tristan fired on instinct.

I was on the floor, face-first in the water-logged carpet. The thumping helicopter blades and blaring siren framed an unexpected silence. My body throbbed. I couldn't feel where the bullet had hit, but I knew it had. I slowly turned my head to the side and opened my eyes. I saw yellow. It took me a second to realize that I was staring right at a rubber ducky, just inches from my face. I pushed it out of the way and looked back. I had been felled by an oar, what a pathetic way to die. To my right, I saw Nick. He lay in a fetal position, his back to me, motionless. In front of me, the horror that was Maxwell's face was on the ground, not more than three feet from my own. There was a red dot between his eyes, a pool of red spreading around him. Maybe the bullet didn't have my name on it after all. The silence was broken by a cascade of boots. "Police! Everybody down!" I rested the side of my head against the floor and let my eyes close.

AFTERMATH

T ristan sat on the rear bumper of an ambulance out on the exhibit parking lot. Strobing emergency vehicles were strewn around the lot like someone had dropped a bucket of Hot Wheels. The cool night air cleared his mind. It would be a while before all the question marks were sorted out. But tonight, the cops had, to his own surprise, and thanks to Maria's and Rajeev's initial statements, let him go on his own recognizance. A medic attended to his leg when an angry Kalminski popped up out of nowhere. She was in leggings and a sports bra again, with an unzipped hoodie to top it off. She had that healthy glow about her.

"Christ, are you constantly working out?" Tristan asked.

"It's Sunday morning, what do you expect?" Kalminski replied, crossing her arms.

"True, although 4 am is mighty early for hill running."

"To get ahead, you need to be ahead."

"Huh... is that from your book? Profound."

"Thanks for starting the only nerd-induced riot in recorded human history. I've got ten injured guards and at least 30 injured nerds. We had to shut the whole production down for at least an hour. That alone cost us in the seven figures, then there is the PR and legal fall out to come."

"On a positive note, a major threat to our national security was stopped, and the only people that died were the ones that deserved it. Maybe something for your PR people to spin? Don't forget you did your part in helping us catch, or rather kill, the bad guys."

"Oh, don't worry, I haven't forgotten."

"Listen, it's been great chatting, but I need to get to General. My friends are there." He turned to the medic in front of him. "Think you could give me a ride?"

They had shot me up with something to take the edge off—something I definitely could get used to. The drugs might explain what happened next. My mom burst into my hospital room. She rushed over to my bedside and hugged me more and harder than she had done in the previous 16 years of our lives together—at least it felt that way. "I thought I had lost you too," she said into my neck as she started to sob. I tried to muster my trusted defenses, but I couldn't resist. Instead, I joined her. The sobbing was epic, almost desperate, with our tears and snot in free flow. As far as I knew, it was the first time we'd cried since my dad was murdered. I didn't know where it would take us, but I knew that something changed between us, right then and there.

"How you holding up?" Tristan said as he limped into Maria's hospital room. Rajeev was on a metal folding chair by her side. Tristan had grabbed some flowers in a vase off the nurses' station and now placed them on the table next to Maria.

"Oh my," she said with a weak smile. "You shouldn't have." She had spunk left in her yet. He took her hand where it lay on the covers and squeezed it gently.

"Rajeev," Tristan said. "I have no flowers for you, but thanks."

"Hey, it's the oath, remember? Just part of the job." He couldn't hide the smidgeon of pride that revealed itself in the corners of his mouth.

"Above and beyond, Rajeev, above and beyond." He turned to go. "Of course, I will have to write you up for failure to follow orders, hero or not." He smiled and was out the door.

Three doors down, a couple of local police officers stood

guard. Tristan nodded towards them. "Fred, Miroslav, thanks for doing this." He'd asked them to come by and guard Lily's room. They were two of the few people he could trust right now, friends from basic training. He knocked, pressed down the handle, and pushed through the door.

It was with some relief we were interrupted by a knock, it had gotten hard to breathe. Skulder stuck his head through the doorway. "I preferred you in that mullet," he said as he approached my bedside, nodding to my mom.

"You sure as hell are an all-around disappointment," I replied meekly.

Anticipating my question, Skulder explained, "Nick is down the hall. His family is with him. It's rough having a gun stuck in your mouth... but given time..."

I shut my eyes as guilt washed over me. "You did good, kid," Tristan said. "Your father would be proud."

I opened my eyes again as he turned to go. "What about the others?"

He turned back. "They have some bruises, relatively unscathed. They wanted to see you, but your doctor put a stop to that."

"Hey... what's your name anyway?"

"It's Tristan. Listen, I have told the investigators to hold back for now... but in the next few weeks, there will be a lot of questions that need answering." He was at the door. "But you rest for now."

They let me go home later that same day. That night, I dreamt of Alphacore again. The dream started the way it always did. I walked through the field of tall grass, and came to the hill where my dad sat under his tree, looking out over the landscape with the wind in his hair. I waved and shouted, and at first, there was no reaction. I shouted again, "I did it, Dad! I got them!" Then it happened. He slowly turned his gaze and his eyes met mine, my world ruptured. I saw on his face, finally, that beautiful smile.

The one I had missed so much. "You are free now! You can go!" I shouted. He waved back and nodded slightly.

The dream started to dissolve. I did all I could to hang on to it. I fought against the awakening in me. But in the end, real life won out again—it always does. I opened my eyes and stared up at the ceiling. It was covered with stars and the moon.

Tristan stepped out into the morning air on Portero Avenue. He couldn't delay his date with destiny at the FBI field office any longer. If his leg had been in better shape, he would have hoofed it over to the offices on Golden Gate Avenue, but as it was, he needed a cab.

Tristan had no idea how far inside the bureau the tentacles of conspiracy reached. He wasn't even sure he could trust his own boss, Richards. The video Rembrandt had given him was pretty hard to dismiss. Simon Lut, CEO of Westcap EnviroTech, was on the run. An international arrest warrant with his name on it had already been issued through Interpol.

He thought of Charlie and realized that he hadn't seen his own daughter in over six months. The room in West Oakland he had prepared for her and the bed she was supposed to sleep in were untouched. Why had he been such a coward? Was he ashamed of what he had become, was that the reason he hadn't fought for her? Instead, he had fought for someone else's daughter.

BABY STEPS

My mom and I were in the kitchen, cups of tea in hand, when the doorbell startled me. My mom was quick to sooth. "The police have a cruiser outside, honey, you're safe here." I wanted to remind her that a cop had tried to kill me just two days ago, but didn't. "Why don't you get that?" she said.

I felt the pull of isolation again, as I did after he died. The need to enter myself and leave the world behind. The difference this time was that I resisted it, I knew better—I hoped. I made my way to the front door and placed my eye against the peephole, and my heart skipped a beat. I turned the deadbolt, took a deep breath, and pulled open the door.

Sarah was in her jogging gear. She held out a small, rectangular, white box. "A phone, for you," she said. "You can't expect me to be coming over once an hour every time I want to talk." I hesitated, then took the box. "Now, before you get all choked up and all, know that it's just a crappy Chinese thing. It's probably bristling with spyware, so be careful what you talk about. You wouldn't want the Chinese government finding out about your gas issues, right?"

"True," I said. "Listen... I just want you to know that I'm—"
Sarah held up her hand. "I don't want to hear it."
"I shouldn't have—"
"Enough. Go and get geared up and let's hit them hills."
I was halfway up the stairs when she called after me from the doorway, "And, Lil, you better not let me win this time."

With my grief, my world had imploded and become infinitely small. I couldn't see, then, that Sarah's world and mine were inexorably tethered, like the steel cables unifying the two towers of the Golden Gate. I thought that I wasn't worthy of her love... I was wrong.

A week later, the crew was chilling in Nick's basement, the four of us just regular noobs. The tournament had continued on without us. The fact that there had been a gun battle a few feet from thousands of clueless gamers didn't seem to phase Alphacore corporate. The show must go on. The advertisers must be given satisfaction. A consolation of sorts was that one of the favorites, a professional outfit out of Seoul, had won, raking home the 200,000-dollar prize. Better that than some other ragtag team of newbies, like us, be given eternal glory.

"Oh, George," Jamaal said, "before you get shipped off to oblivion, you'll need to hand over keys to the Twitch account." George's parents were going to send him off to another rehab, this time for three whole weeks somewhere in the middle of the woods without electricity and barely any running water. The second-degree burns on his nipples were the tipping point.

"What are our numbers?" I asked, actually interested for once.

"We've hit the 100,000 mark," Jamaal said. "We could almost live off that now. We wouldn't need that bitcoin of yours." He was referring to the stash my dad had left me—we hadn't figured out what to do with that just yet.

Changing the subject, Nick said, "Listen, guys, we fought good and hard," taking back his role as team leader. "We gave them hell in both worlds." Nick was almost back to his good old self, but something in his eyes had changed. They were the eyes of a grown man... a man who had stared death in the face, twice. He was seeing a shrink. They'd wanted me to see one too, but I'd refused. I hadn't felt this good since before my dad was killed, and wasn't sure if it was ok.

"We'll take them next year," I said, tagging onto Nick's optimistic note.

"Interesting that you should say that," Nick said. "Our performance—"

"Lily's performance," George clarified.

"Our *team* performance got us noticed. When I opened my email earlier today, guess what I found?"

"Spit it out, Nick," I said.

"An invitation to the hottest invitational of the spring."

"That's a good thing... right?" Jamaal ventured, picking up on Nick's muted enthusiasm.

"One slight detail that I should mention," Nick continued. "The tournament is in St. Petersburg."

"I see your point," George said. "Miami would be sweeter. But there are worse things than Florida in spring."

"St. Petersburg, Russia, you dope," Nick said.

We fell silent for a moment, contemplating the implications.

"What now?" Nick wondered, finally, not really expecting an answer.

"I know exactly what we need," I said. I whipped out my phone, the one Sarah had given me. "I just need to make a call."

The boys squealed like piglets as I gunned the twin 150 HP Yamahas and the boat lifted out of the water. We were in the Rib Craft again, it felt like ages ago, even if it had only been weeks. "Enjoy," Sylvester had said as he threw me the keys when JRN showed up at the dock of the club. There was no need to steal this time around. The sun skipped across the cobalt ocean and the Rib Craft thumped in the water, made choppy by the afternoon breeze. It was cold out on the water, so we were all bulked up with borrowed heavy-duty sailing jackets.

I knew what the boat could take, but the boys clearly didn't. When I spotted a particularly large swell, I smiled and pressed the gas lever to the max. The boat hit the wave and took off, the outboard motors groaned as the propellers lifted out of the water and we were completely airborne. For a few seconds, the squeals turned to dreaded silence as Nick, George, and Jamaal lifted off the deck and they too became airborne, with their white-knuckled fists on the guardrail being the only thing keeping them from falling into oblivion. The bow crashed into the next wave and the boys crashed into the deck. A few seconds passed as they checked if they were still alive, and then came a burst of hysterical laughter as they realized that they were still breathing—they were still nerds at heart after all.

The club leadership had magnanimously reinstated our membership. While the mayhem at the boat exhibit had made the national news, no journalist knew the whole story. What did eventually become clear to everyone was that my dad had been framed. He was innocent and had been murdered for doing the right, even heroic, thing. I felt the tug of the ocean, but it just wasn't the same anymore. I knew that this time would be the last time I set foot at the club.

Later that evening, I was, with some relief, holding Nick's father's hand at the dinner table. I hadn't been sure that I was welcome back to their table after I'd almost gotten their son's head blown off. To my right, I was holding a new hand. I squeezed that hand, and it squeezed me back.

Nick's father started to speak: "May we be grateful—"

"Can I?" I asked, leaning in. "May I? This time?" Nick's dad simply smiled and nodded.

In my mind, I had prepared something stirring and profound, but whatever it was, it had evaporated like water on Arizona blacktop in high summer. I looked at those around me, Abby, Nick's mom and dad, Nick with those blue eyes, and finally, I looked at my mom. When Nick first suggested I bring my mom to the thanksgiving dinner, various scenes of disaster and embarrassment flashed before my eyes. My mom drinking herself into oblivion and passing out on top of the turkey was one such scene.

Then I thought of what my dad would have wanted me to do. The last thing, literally, he ever said to me was to go easy on my mom, that she was trying. I looked to my right. My mom looked back at me with anticipation and pride, and maybe love. Most of my cornerstone memories were memories of my dad. My mom was hardly there at all, an undefined presence, hovering in the background like an extra on a movie set. Could I build new memories with her by my side? I glanced down at the broccoli on my plate, closed my eyes and inhaled.

* * * * *

THANK YOU

Thank you for finishing my book.

I hope you've enjoyed *As Worlds Drifted*. Finding an audience as a newbie novelist can be tough. You would really be helping me out if you could head on over to Amazon and submit a quick review. One or two lines is plenty. By leaving a review on Amazon you will help others find *As Worlds Drifted*.

If you would like to join my newsletter to recieve updates on when other formats of the book are available, you can go to parkertiden.com

You can also connect with me on Facebook

https://www.facebook.com/parkertiden

Parker

Printed in Great Britain
by Amazon

57896736R00120